Kidnapped!

"You stole Jenny," said Carey. It was not what she had intended to say at all.

The gray-faced man grew grayer still. "You're right, in a way," he said in a voice that was almost a whisper. "Though I didn't steal her, I know where she is. I'll take you there. But you've got to keep your mouth shut on the way. Any hollering or bawling or yelling and the deal is off. Understand?"

"I guess." Carey trembled. Then, without knowing how it happened, she found herself being half-lifted, half-pushed into the high seat of the van. A second later, the gray man was in beside her at the wheel.

"Head down and your mouth shut," he said, "or you won't see Jenny."

Books by Jeannette Eyerly

HE'S MY BABY NOW
IF I LOVED YOU WEDNESDAY
MORE THAN A SUMMER LOVE
THE PHAEDRA COMPLEX
RADIGAN CARES
THE SEEING SUMMER

Available from ARCHWAY paperbacks

The Seeing Summer

Jeannette Eyerly

illustrated by Emily Arnold McCully

AN ARCHWAY PAPERBACK
Published by POCKET BOOKS • NEW YORK

The Author Is a Member of the Authors League of America

An Archway Paperback published by
POCKET BOOKS, a division of Simon & Schuster, Inc.
1230 Avenue of the Americas, New York, N.Y. 10020

Published by arrangement with J. B. Lippincott Company,
Junior Books, a Division of Harper & Row Publishers, Inc.
Library of Congress Catalog Card Number: 81-47440

ISBN: 0-671-45661-X

First Archway Paperback printing August, 1984

10 9 8 7 6 5 4 3

AN ARCHWAY PAPERBACK and colophon are
registered trademarks of Simon & Schuster, Inc.

Printed in the U.S.A.

IL 3+

For Kenneth Jernigan
with admiration and affection

"The real problem of blindness is not the loss of eyesight. The real problem is the misunderstanding and lack of information which exist. If a blind person has proper training and if he has opportunity, blindness is only a physical nuisance."

—*Kenneth Jernigan*

The author is grateful to Dr. Wallace and Mrs. Ruth Schroeder, Shirley Lansing, and Doris M. Willoughby for their wise counsel and careful reading of the manuscript.

A great deal is owed to the scores of blind persons, young and old, who became her friends during her service with the Iowa Commission for the Blind.

Contents

The Seeing Summer

1

The House Next Door

Hopping on one foot, Carey glared at the chunk of cement that had worked its way up from a crack in the sidewalk. Tears came to her eyes—not because of pain, though her toe did hurt a lot, but from disappointment.

Aunt Richard had warned her, too.

At breakfast only that morning, Aunt Richard had said, "Now, Carey, don't get your hopes up. Just because it's the last day of school and you *dreamed* somebody bought the house next door, doesn't mean it's going to happen. Run along to school like a good girl and get your report card. When you come home, we'll find something interesting to do."

But Carey's dream of the night before was so real, she paid no attention. Right up to the minute she sped around the corner, report card in her hand and her book bag jouncing, she expected to see a big moving truck in front of the house next door. There was another part of her dream that she had not told Aunt Richard. She expected to see a girl just her age sitting on the steps, just as she had seen her in her dream.

Instead, the blue and white real estate sign still stood where it had been planted in the front yard the day her best friend, Debra Denman, had moved away.

Now, Carey was sure no one would ever buy the house. Even after she grew up, got married, and had a baby, the house would still be standing empty.

She could not understand why no one wanted it. Older than the one she lived in, it had an attic you could explore, a screened-in porch across the front, and a bay window in the dining room. On one side of the house, a monkey swing dangled from a high branch of an oak tree. On the other side was an apple tree good for climbing, and the good-sized hole she and Debra had started digging for a swimming pool.

Limping a little in case anyone should be looking, and with her head down, Carey walked past the empty house. She did not want to be reminded of all the good times she and Debra Denman had had playing there.

The long summer vacation stretched away with no one to play with but Pansy Prugh, who was only eight, told lies, and wore her old dancing costumes to play in.

As Carey came into the cool, dark front hall of her own house and the screen door sucked quietly shut behind her, Aunt Richard called out, "Here I am! In the kitchen!"

Aunt Richard was not really an aunt. Carey's father had got her out of a want ad right after her mother died, and she'd lived with them ever since. Giving Carey a floury pat, and the loaf of bread she was

2

kneading a sharp slap, Aunt Richard said, "Isn't it wonderful?"

Carey reached out and swiftly picked off a small twist of dough—a practice Aunt Richard did not approve of—and ate it. "Isn't what wonderful?"

"Why, about the house next door," said Aunt Richard. "I thought you would notice the first thing as you came home from school."

"I noticed the sign was still there," said Carey, looking glum. "I saw that the minute I came around the corner."

"Well," said Aunt Richard. "I think you had better take another look."

Out the front door and across the side yard in a flash, Carey suddenly stopped. What could Aunt Richard have been thinking of? It was not like her to make jokes. The sign was still there, just as she thought.

But wait, thought Carey, slowly approaching. There *was* a difference. Pasted slantwise across the top of the words For Sale was the single beautiful word Sold!

Back home in a minute, Carey banged through to the kitchen. "Who bought it?" she demanded. "What is their name? When are they moving in? Do they . . . do they have any kids?"

"One question at a time," said Aunt Richard, trying to look severe and failing. "And I'll tell you everything I know. Not more than an hour ago the real estate lady came over to use the telephone. She told me the house was bought by a family named Lee who are moving here from out of state. And, yes, they do have children. A baby boy and a girl of ten."

"Ten!" cried Carey. She grabbed Aunt Richard

around her plump middle and tried to dance her around.

"Carey!" shrilled Aunt Richard. "Stop! Stop! This instant. And calm yourself."

Carey stopped dancing Aunt Richard around. But she could not calm herself. She was too excited.

Carey spent the rest of the afternoon cleaning her room. She did not want her new friend—for they would be best friends in no time at all—to see what a mess it was in.

She hung up the clothes that were on the floor of her closet and rearranged the furniture in the dollhouse she hardly ever played with anymore. She straightened her bookcase, putting all ten of her Linda Fairweather, Girl Detective, mysteries in a row. If her new friend had not read them, she would lend them to her. She polished the glass on the picture of the pretty mother she had never known, tidied her desk drawers and the top of her dresser. She threw away a dead turtle. Instead of becoming a fossil, it had started to smell. She printed WELCOME TO THE NAYBERHOOD in large letters on a piece of cardboard, put a border of flowers around it, and fastened it to her bulletin board.

Then, though Aunt Richard had told her she had no idea when the new family would be moving in, she settled down to watch and wait.

From her upstairs window nearest her bed, she had a perfect view of the street, the driveway, and the empty house itself. Whatever happened, she would see it.

While she waited, she thought about all the interesting things she and her new friend would do together.

4

Swing on the monkey swing, pretending they were trapeze artists with the circus. They would climb the apple tree, perhaps build a tree house. They would ride their bicycles over to the park and go to the ice cream store in the shopping center. On nice days they would have picnics and on rainy days they might give a play in the attic.

Carey turned her gaze from the window back to her room. The dark green carpet, rose-sprigged wallpaper, and white ruffly curtains looked so much nicer when the room was picked up.

Only one thing was missing. Flowers.

Carey had just started to pick some daisies from the perennial garden that divided her own backyard from Pansy Prugh's, when Pansy minced out her back door. She was wearing her fairy costume.

Slowly waving her gauze wings, which were fastened to her arms, she pointed her wand at Carey.

"What are you doing?" she said in a thin piercing voice. "I command you to tell me."

Carey did not reply.

Pansy lowered her voice and, changing it to a whine, said, "Well, what are you doing?"

"Picking flowers. For my room," said Carey.

"Why?"

"Because," said Carey. She found it every bit as difficult to talk to Pansy as to play with her. She snapped off a daisy without a stem.

"Because why?" persisted Pansy. "Is someone coming over?"

"Maybe not today," said Carey, "but soon." Then, because she could not contain the exciting news any

5

longer, she said, "A new family is moving into the house next door."

"Oh, *them*." Pansy's voice was creamy with satisfaction. "I know all about *them*. My father told me. Their name is Lee, and they're rich. Dr. Lee wouldn't even have to work if he didn't want to. But he does. He's a scientist or something. He's going to work at the university."

Carey went on picking flowers.

"But that's not all," said Pansy, with the air of one who saves the best to the last. "Besides a new baby, there's a girl who's older than me, who's blind."

"An older—What?"

"A girl who's blind. She was born that way. When she was a baby her parents took her to famous doctors everywhere, but they couldn't do anything about it. So if you're picking flowers for her, it won't do you any good."

"I don't believe you!" cried Carey.

"You don't need to believe me," said Pansy. "You'll find out. My father is a newspaper editor and he knows *everything*." With that remark, spoken in her most piercing voice, she rose on her toes and pointed her wand at Carey. "I command you to tell no one. If you do, you shall be turned to stone."

Her heart beating fast, Carey turned to go in the house. She didn't believe for a minute the new girl was blind. It was just one of Pansy's stories. Like the one she told about going to the White House in her mother's stomach and meeting the President of the United States and his wife. Or the small rock Pansy insisted an astronaut had picked up on the moon.

To prove she didn't believe what Pansy said, Carey

put the flowers she'd picked in a cheese glass full of water.

But what if . . . ? What if the new girl really couldn't see them? What if she couldn't see the sign WEL-COME TO THE NAYBERHOOD? Or see how tidy the dollhouse was? Or how neatly she had arranged Linda Fairweather, Girl Detective, in her bookcase? What if she couldn't see to read?

That would be worst of all.

Carey dug her fists into her eyes until they blos-somed with sprinkles of rainbow-colored dots and streamers. She tried to imagine what it would be like if she couldn't see.

But not that day, the next day, or the day after that, did she tell anyone what Pansy Prugh had said. Not until she saw the new girl walking around and bumping into things would she believe that she was blind.

Carey kept watch on the house next door from her front steps and from the window of her upstairs bed-room.

And Aunt Richard kept watch on Carey.

"You haven't a temperature, I'd swear to that," said Aunt Richard, laying the back of her fingers across Carey's forehead. "Are you sure you feel all right?"

Carey wanted to twitch off Aunt Richard's fingers and say, "Leave me alone!", but she did not. She loved Aunt Richard and did not want to hurt her feelings. Besides, Aunt Richard could not help being a fussbudget. In fact, that is what she sometimes called herself. She made little laughing apologies for being worried when Carey, dawdling on the way, was late coming home from school. Once, the summer before, when she and Debra Denman had walked home from the branch library, they had been so busy reading they had missed three buses in a row! That time, Aunt Richard admitted she had been on the verge of calling the police.

So when Aunt Richard felt Carey's forehead and asked her if she felt all right, Carey said she did. And when Aunt Richard said, "Then why don't you run outdoors and play," Carey said she would after a while.

Wearing her worried expression, Aunt Richard went back downstairs saying, "I wish the child's father weren't out of town."

The next morning when Carey woke up she looked out her bedroom window at a yellow station wagon parked in the driveway of the house next door. Behind it was a moving van.

From it, with astonishing speed, two men started removing large bulky objects wrapped in old comforters. There was a grand piano and dining room table without any legs. A stove, refrigerator, a baby bed, mattresses, a desk, more beds, all kinds of chairs and a sofa. Then came boxes, barrels, and crates. Dozens and dozens of them.

Just before the moving van pulled away, a man wandered out on the porch. He was as tall as her father, but thinner. A little later, a woman wearing jeans and a man's white shirt with the sleeves rolled up and the shirttails tied in front, appeared. She was carrying a baby.

But where was the girl?

Could the real estate lady and Pansy's father have made a mistake? Was it possible there was no girl? For a moment, Carey felt almost relieved. Better there be no girl than one who was blind.

And, perhaps, Carey thought, if that was the case she might "baby-sit" the baby. Lisl Gardner, who lived down the street and who, according to Aunt Richard, was "eleven, going on twenty-five," baby-sat her little sister all the time. Or so she said.

A vision of herself arriving for work at the Lees' front door crossed Carey's mind. She would be dressed in white because white was so sanitary, and she would carry a first-aid kit. Just in case.

But the vision disappeared as the front door again opened and a little white cane appeared. Holding it before her and swinging it back and forth in an arc, was a girl just Carey's size.

Carey had seen enough. As tears came to her eyes, she ran to the bed and threw herself down on the pillow.

Aunt Richard tapped lightly on the closed door of Carey's bedroom. "Pansy Prugh is here. She wants you to come out and play."

"I don't want to," said Carey in a muffled voice. "Tell her to go home."

"I'm afraid I can't do that," Aunt Richard replied. "That would be rude. If you want Pansy to go home, you will have to tell her yourself."

Carey got up from her bed where she had been lying with her blanket sucking her thumb. This was something she didn't do very often—only when things were going very badly indeed, and then only in secret. Of course, Aunt Richard and her father knew she still had her "bankie," of which only a small piece of satin binding and a few miserable knitted woolen shreds

9

remained. Aunt Richard carefully washed it now and then, putting it in a net bag to protect it. This was an act Carey very much appreciated.

Sometimes Carey thought her father suspected she still sucked her thumb. Once, after she'd been sent to her room for punishment, he had taken her right hand and remarked that her thumb looked a little softer and a little cleaner than her fingers. That was all he said. But with Easter approaching, she had given up her thumb for the rest of Lent.

Knowing that Aunt Richard was still patiently waiting outside her door to see what she would do, Carey stuffed her bankie's remains under the pillow and went downstairs.

From inside the house, Carey could see Pansy standing on the front porch looking in through the big front window. She was wearing shiny, bright blue satin shorts, a blouse with shiny things that looked like fish scales sewed all over it, and her tap-dancing shoes.

Going out on the porch, Carey said, "I can't play," before Pansy had a chance to say a word.

"Well, neither can she," said Pansy, tossing her head in the direction of the Lee house, "but you wouldn't believe me." With that, she went tappety-tap, tappety-tap, tappety-tap-tap-tap down the front sidewalk. There she made a sweeping bow and ran as fast as she could toward home.

2

The Bisness Book

"There are lots of things a blind person can do," said Aunt Richard.

"What kind of things?" asked Carey.

"Well, for one thing, they are usually *very* good in music. There are, I believe, some rather famous blind musicians."

"But not when they are ten years old," said Carey. She never felt as cross as when Aunt Richard was trying to be reasonable.

"Perhaps not at ten," Aunt Richard admitted. "But later. I remember a blind man came to tune our piano when I was a child. His wife brought him. She gave me and my sister music lessons." Aunt Richard's brow wrinkled in concentration. "And don't forget Helen Keller. And besides her, there are many, many other people who have succeeded in spite of handicaps."

"I know," said Carey. "But I don't want them living

next door to me. I don't want to have to play with them."

"I'm afraid you are acting very badly," said Aunt Richard, who though not a mother often sounded like one. "It's been two whole days since the Lees moved in and you have not made the first move to get acquainted."

"There's no use in getting acquainted," said Carey. "There won't be anything we can do."

"Carey!" This time, Aunt Richard spoke in a voice that meant no more arguing. "If nothing else, you can offer to read to the poor child. Just think how you would feel if you were blind and moving into a strange neighborhood."

That is exactly what Carey *had* been thinking, and she couldn't stand it.

"So I suggest you go over there right now," said Aunt Richard briskly. "I've just taken a batch of cookies out of the oven. You can take a nice plateful over to the Lees. That will help break the ice."

There was nothing else for Carey to do but go. Instead of cutting across the two side yards, she took the long way down the sidewalk. Because Aunt Richard was watching her, she walked slowly. However, now that she was on her way she was glad she was going. She was curious.

The new girl was sitting on the front steps of her house. Carey stopped a few feet away to study her. She wondered how it would feel to have someone look at you when you couldn't look at them.

Like Carey, the new girl was wearing shorts, a shirt with a little alligator on the pocket, and sandals. But while Carey's fly-away reddish hair was so curly it

made the ends of her twin braids turn up, the other's hair was a smooth dark brown. It was cut with bangs. The sides came down a little longer than the bottom of her ears.

Carey moved a few steps closer to peer at her eyes. They were brown, with thick black lashes. Except for a small pinpoint of light at the very center, which was different, they didn't look strange at all. She had worried about that.

Although she had been very young, not more than three or four, she still remembered the old man sitting in a camp chair on a downtown street corner selling pencils. Dragging on Aunt Richard's hand, she had wanted to look at the pencils but had, instead, looked into the old man's eyes. Bluish gray, they looked as if someone had spilled milk into them and stirred it all around.

"What is the matter with his eyes?" she had asked, even before they had moved a step away.

Aunt Richard had loudly said, "Shush!" then in a lower voice had said, "He's blind."

Later, Aunt Richard had explained how never, ever should she mention anything unusual about another person. And that she never, ever stare. Like she was doing now.

Carey cleared her throat. "HELLO."

"I'm not deaf," said the new girl. She looked at Carey just as if she could see her. "You needn't YELL."

"I didn't yell," said Carey. She was so taken by surprise her voice came out in a little squeak.

"Yes, you did. When people first know you're blind, they always yell. They think because you can't see, you can't hear either."

14

"Well, if I yelled, I'm sorry," said Carey in a voice so low she could scarcely hear it herself. "I came over to get acquainted. I live next door. My name is Carey Cramer."

"My name is Jenny Anne Lee, but I like to be called plain Jenny. I'm ten, just like you are. The real estate lady told me that. And you don't need to stare, either."

"I'm not!" Again Carey spoke too loudly, because that is exactly what she had been doing.

"Yes, you were," said Jenny. "I can tell. I can feel you."

Carey did not like Jenny saying that at all. It was spooky. She scrubbed the toe of her sneaker over the sidewalk and shot a quick look at the new girl.

But what she did next was spookier still. "You brought something over. Something to eat. What is it?"

"Coo-cookies," stammered Carey. "How did you know?"

"Because I smelled them. Don't be stupid," Jenny said. "Chocolate chip?"

"That's *very* good," said Carey approvingly. Even though Jenny had called her stupid, she knew she hadn't meant it that way. Now that the mystery was explained, she could smell the cookies herself.

"I was beginning to think," she added lamely, "that you weren't, well . . ." She waited so long to say the terrible word *blind* that Jenny finished it for her.

"Blind, blind, BLIND!" Jenny said. "So what?" She stuck her chin out in a most alarming way.

"So, nothing."

"Why didn't you want to say blind, then?"

"I, I don't know," Carey said. She took a couple of steps backward down the sidewalk.

"Yes, you do," said Jenny, scowling. "You think blind is bad."

Tears made Carey's eyes smart. What a hateful girl! Pansy Prugh was almost perfect in comparison.

"Well, maybe I do," Carey said, "but I think mean is worse!" Winking back tears, she ran across the side yards toward her house.

Not until she was almost at her own front door did she remember she was still carrying the plate of cookies! What to do? She could not tell Aunt Richard the Lees were not at home, because she had seen Jenny sitting on her front steps. She couldn't say Mrs. Lee had said, "Thank you very much, but we do not care for chocolate chip cookies." No, there was nothing to do but go back and give them to the horrid Jenny before Aunt Richard came out and wanted to know what was going on.

Jenny was still sitting on her front steps when Carey returned.

"Here are your old cookies," Carey said, in a voice so low it was not more than a whisper. "I forgot to give them to you."

"If you hadn't come back, I was going over to your house and say *I* was sorry, but sometimes when people yell or stare or feel sorry for me it makes me mad."

Not looking terribly sorry, in Carey's opinion, Jenny hopped to her feet. "Come on," she said. "You can carry the cookies, if you want."

Mrs. Lee was standing on a chair hanging curtains in the living room.

"Mom," said Jenny. "This is Carey Cramer. She lives next door. Look what she brought us."

"How nice!" exclaimed Mrs. Lee, who had dark brown hair like Jenny's and bright brown eyes. She looked very lively and friendly. "Thank your mother very much."

"My mother didn't make them. My Aunt Richard did," said Carey, politely. "My mother's dead and my Aunt Richard is not my aunt at all but the lady who's taken care of me since I was born."

"Oh, my dear, I am sorry," said Mrs. Lee, getting down from the chair. "I didn't know about your mother."

"Oh, that's all right," said Carey, kindly. Which it was. Almost everyone, the minute they heard her mother was dead, looked as if they were going to cry. Sometimes, if things were not going well for her, Carey would bring it into the conversation herself. This usually proved quite effective.

Mrs. Lee, however, seemed to recover more quickly than most. "Well, then, thank your Aunt Richard. I hope to meet her soon, but I won't be doing very much visiting for a while yet." She laughed. "As you can see, we're still in pretty much of a mess."

Carey looked around. The grand piano, which she had seen coming in the door, now had its legs on. She remembered what Aunt Richard had said about the blind being musical, so it must be Jenny's piano.

Carey herself was not musical. Though she had started taking lessons when she was six, she had been allowed to give them up because her father said she had a "tin ear," whatever that was.

The dining room table was also wearing its legs and was standing in place. So was a nice fat sofa and a number of other large pieces of furniture. A lot of boxes and barrels still remained to be unpacked, and pictures were stacked against the walls. It was not at these things, however, that Carey was really looking. She wanted to see if Pansy Prugh had been right about the Lees being rich. Perhaps there might be some finger bowls sitting about. Finger bowls were the one certain sign of richness with which she was acquainted. She had been given one by a servant at the conclusion of a dinner party she and her father had been invited to in New York City. It had sat on a lace doily and had a slice of lemon floating in it.

If the Lees did have finger bowls, thought Carey, they were probably not yet unpacked. Aloud she said, "I think you're coming along very nicely."

Mrs. Lee laughed. "Oh, we'll get there." She came down from the chair. "My," she exclaimed, "those cookies look delicious! And such a pretty plate. But it mustn't get broken in all our confusion. Jenny, why don't you take it to the kitchen and put the cookies on one of our plates? Then Carey can take hers home with her when she goes."

Jenny made her way to the kitchen as easily as she had made her way through the cluttered living room.

Carey, wondering how she did it, followed close behind. She knew, however, that Jenny would soon need help. The twist-'em on the plastic bag that enclosed the plate of cookies was fastened tightly. She had put it on herself. It would be hard to undo. And it wouldn't be easy to transfer the cookies from one plate to another without spilling them.

"I'll take that twist-'em thing off the plastic bag for you," said Carey, generously pushing forward and reaching for the cookie plate.

"*I'll* take it off," said Jenny. And she did. With no more trouble than Carey would have had. From a cupboard at one side of the sink, she got a plate. She slid the cookies on it, popped the whole thing back in the plastic bag, and was fastening the tie when Mrs. Lee came out in the kitchen.

"I'm going to run up to that hardware store at the mall and see if I can get some drapery hooks. The baby's so fussy, I'm taking him. Maybe the ride will put him to sleep. In any case, I won't be long—twenty minutes or so." She looked brightly around. "Oh, another thing. Jenny, if you'd like, you can stir up a package of pudding. Chocolate or butterscotch, I don't care. They're there on the counter. Either will go nicely with the cookies Carey brought over. If you put the pudding in individual dishes and put them in the refrigerator, it should be cold by dinnertime."

So many instructions! thought Carey. Surely Mrs. Lee would not have left Jenny alone to make pudding if she, Carey, were not there to help her.

"Which pudding do you want?" asked Carey helpfully. "I'll open it for you."

"Chocolate," said Jenny. "And *I'll* open it."

Carey watched closely as Jenny chose the right package. How did she do it? As far as Carey could see, all she did was run her fingers over the front of it. Just as skillfully, she took down a medium-sized saucepan from the wall above the stove and said, "You can help, if you like. You can get the milk from the refrigerator."

Yes, thought Carey. *Getting* the milk. And *pouring*

it. And *turning on the stove*—a quick glance showed her it was almost exactly like the one she had at home—*and* stirring it and finally pouring it in the dishes.

By the time Carey got the milk from the refrigerator, Jenny had the measuring cup already on the counter.

"I'd better pour it," she said in a loud voice. "You might spill."

Jenny said, "You're yelling again. And I won't spill any more than you will. Give me the milk."

Carey let Jenny take it. After all, it was her house. However, she did hope with all her heart that Jenny would spill. Not a lot. Not enough to make a terrible mess—that would be mean—but *some*.

As it turned out, Jenny only spilled about a teaspoonful.

Carey had to admire how Jenny did it. Carefully holding the cup, she slowly poured the milk until it touched the tip of her finger. She poured another cup the same way.

Carey would have liked to pour the milk into the chocolate powder but Jenny had already put it in the saucepan and was busily stirring. She also noticed that Jenny had turned the stove on to "low." She knew this was the proper temperature to cook the pudding, but with so many different settings on the dial of the stove, how did Jenny know which was which?

It was boring, standing there doing nothing. She and Debra had always taken turns at everything.

Presently she said, "I have to go home now."

Jenny turned from the stove. "Well, I *am* pretty busy," she said. "And thanks for the cookies. See you tomorrow."

As Carey left, she somehow managed to bump into the frame of the kitchen door, giving her forehead a nasty crack. Tears were flooding her eyes as she dashed toward home.

Aunt Richard met her at the door. "I'm glad you stayed to play a while, Carey. That was good of you."

"We didn't play," mumbled Carey.

Aunt Richard sighed. "I suppose not. There's probably not much the child can do."

Make pudding, thought Carey.

That night after supper, while Aunt Richard watched her favorite TV program—each night she had a different "favorite"—Carey went up to her room. She decided she didn't like Jenny at all.

However, even if she liked Jenny and wanted to talk to her, she couldn't do it. An hour before, the whole Lee family had gone somewhere in their car.

Carey shut the door and sat on the edge of her bed where she could look out the window at the house next door. Little by little, it was glimmering away in the approaching darkness.

Soon she wouldn't be able to see the house at all. It made her shiver to think that was the way her house looked to Jenny all the time.

A little later Aunt Richard, making little wheezing noises, came upstairs. She paused outside Carey's door.

"Carey," she said, "have you gone to bed? And if you haven't, what in the world are you doing in there in the dark?"

"Nothing," said Carey.

"Then I suggest you either turn on the light and do

21

something or go to bed. The way you have been acting isn't healthy. I swear to goodness."

"I'll turn on the light," said Carey, with a sigh loud enough for Aunt Richard to hear.

She got up from the bed, fumbled for the switch on her Bo-Peep lamp that wore a flounced lampshade for a skirt. CRASH! Off went the lamp on the floor. And off went the cheese glass of flowers, now withered, she had picked days before in celebration of the arrival of the new girl.

"I trust it's not broken, whatever it is," said Aunt Richard from outside the door.

Carey, who meantime had found another light to turn on, inspected the damage. "The cheese glass didn't break," she said, "but Bo-Peep broke her arm a bit and the light bulb . . . it's in about a million pieces."

She waited a second and when Aunt Richard just wheezed a bit louder, Carey said, "You can come in, if you want to."

One of the good things about Aunt Richard: she never went on making you feel bad when you felt terrible already. Instead of scolding, she told Carey to get a broom, dustpan, and some wet paper towels to pick up the tiniest glass pieces.

After Aunt Richard cleaned up the mess and rescued Bo-Peep's elbow, she said, "Don't worry, sweetie. I can glue this back in place so it will never show. And you mustn't worry about that poor child next door, either."

She gave Carey a little hug, told her to sleep tight and that as soon as she watched the ten o'clock news she was going to bed.

That was the second time that day Aunt Richard had called Jenny a "poor child." Carey was glad Jenny hadn't heard her say it. It would make her mad. Without meaning to, *she* had made Jenny mad twice that day. It was while she was wondering how to get along with anyone so difficult—she had never had any trouble with Debra—she remembered the Bisness Book.

The Bisness Book was a spiral notebook she and Debra had bought at a neighborhood garage sale the summer before for fifteen cents. They tore out the pages that had funny writing on them, which made it as good as new.

If Aunt Richard ever found the Bisness Book Carey did not know what she would do. The first thing in the book was something about Aunt Richard. Something not very nice.

That was why the book had to be so carefully hidden. She got it out from under the mattress of her bed. It looked just as it had when she saw it last. That was three months ago when Debra moved away.

Written on the cover in black marking pencil, in her best block letters, were the words BISNESS BOOK. Underneath this was printed, "Whoever Finds This Book and Looks Inside It Will Die."

On the first page, Debra had written in her plump but very clear cursive backhand:

Carey's Aunt Richard has a mousetash.

This was true, of course. It was soft and a light brown in color. And, of course, Aunt Richard knew she had it. About once a month, she would appear at breakfast wearing a white smelly smear on her upper lip. This made the mustache go away for a while.

Even so, it was nothing to be talked about. Therefore the Bisness Book seemed to be the proper place to make note of it.

The next item in the book was in her own hand.

Debra saw Daryl Johnson going to the toilet in a bush on the way home from school.

Although Debra said you couldn't see anything but Daryl Johnson's back, she knew what he was doing because she had a brother. This entry did not seem as shocking as when she put it in the Bisness Book, but she still wished she had been there to see what there was to see.

The item about Miss Purvis, the art teacher, Carey had written.

When Miss Purvis wears her blue dress and leans over your desk you can see her lungs.

She and Debra had both known it was Miss Purvis's bosoms and not her lungs you could see, but even in the Bisness Book *lungs* seemed to be a better word. But either way, lungs or bosoms, it was something you did not want to talk about. Certainly not in front of Aunt Richard or any of the boys at school.

The next and final item she had also written.

In math, Carey saw Chuck Smithers cheat.

Though both she and Debra had wanted to tell Mrs. Lewis, they'd kept the dreadful knowledge to themselves.

Reading and remembering, Carey sighed. She felt cross. Although she and Debra had promised to be friends forever, neither of them had written after their very first letters crossed in the mail!

Scowling, she printed "THE END" after the last entry and moved down a space. Chewing the end of her pencil and continuing to scowl, Carey wrote:

BLIND PEEPLE

1. *Don't yell at them. They aren't deff.*
2. *Don't stare at them. They can feel you doing it and they don't like it.*
3. *Don't try to help them do anything if they think they can do it themselves. Sometimes they can.*

Carey had barely finished when she heard the Lees come home. She turned out the light and looked out the window. Mr. Lee had put the car in the garage at the back of the house, and now the family was trooping around to the front. Mr. Lee was whistling. Mrs. Lee's bright voice carried clearly on the night air. Jenny was laughing.

Carey undressed in the dark, to see what it would be like. How any of the Lees could be happy, she did not understand.

3

Hell-oooo! Hall-oooo!

The next morning when Carey got up, her father was sitting at the kitchen table, drinking coffee.

Aunt Richard, who was across from him, said, "Look who's here! Look who blew in from Denver this morning before either you or I was awake!"

"Daddy!" cried Carey. She hurled herself across the room into his lap and curled herself up like a dormouse.

He gave her a kiss, rubbing the tip of his nose back and forth across hers. "Hi ya, Pumpkin. Glad to see you."

"Glad to see *you*," Carey said, and gave him the same kind of kiss in return. "Did you win your case?"

"Sure thing," he said.

They grinned at each other.

The two looked remarkably alike—considering one was a grown man and the other a ten-year-old girl. Both had gray-green eyes—Aunt Richard called them

26

"hazel"—curly, copper-colored hair, and short noses with a tilt to them. The chief difference between them was that Thomas Cramer's complexion was ruddy. Carey had inherited from her black-haired, dark-eyed mother a skin that made her as brown as a nut as soon as the sun turned on its tanning rays.

"You've been a good girl?"

Carey looked at Aunt Richard. "Have I? Medium good, maybe?"

"Perhaps medium plus," said Aunt Richard, after pretending to give the matter a lot of thought.

"That's quite good enough," said Carey's father. "Children who are too good are a bore. Now, tell me about the new family next door. Aunt Richard tells me that Mr. Lee is a scientist. A biologist, I believe, who's engaged in some kind of important research at the university. There is also a baby—a boy, I believe—and a girl about your age who is blind."

Carey looked from her father to Aunt Richard, then back to her father. Though both faces looked innocent, Carey guessed they had been talking about the way she had been acting.

She was sure of it when her father said, "When I get home tonight I hope you will be able to tell me you have made some effort to become acquainted with the new girl next door."

Carey did not even try to contain her sigh. If her father wanted her to play with Jenny Lee, she supposed she would have to do it. But she was not looking forward to it.

After Carey had had her breakfast and gone up to her room to get dressed, she saw Jenny looking out the

27

window of her bedroom. Well, maybe not looking out, but standing there looking as if she were looking out. She wondered if, at this distance, Jenny could tell she was staring. She thought it possible.

With this in mind, she opened the screen on her window, stuck her head out, and in a loud voice called, "Hello!"

"Hello!" said Jenny Lee, right back to her.

Then from a distance, faint but still quite shrill, came another "Hall-oooo!"

Leaning out her window as far as she could without falling out, Jenny turned toward the sound of the last "Hall-oooo." "Who was that? It didn't sound exactly like an echo."

Carey hesitated. It had to be Pansy Prugh. How it could be, Carey did not know. The Prugh house was more than twice as far away as her house was from Jenny's.

"Who *was* that?" repeated Jenny in a loud, clear voice. "Does someone else our age live around here?"

Although Pansy was certain to hear anything she said, Carey had no choice but to reply. Keeping her voice as low as possible she said, "Just a person."

"No, I'm not," said this person in penetrating tones. "I am Pansy Anne Prugh. My father is the editor of the *Riverville Daily Record* and my ears are very sharp. This is a free country and I can hear every word you say."

"This is also a dumb conversation," said Jenny. She sounded disgusted. "As soon as I get dressed, I'll come over. O.K.? I'll hurry."

"I'll hurry, too," said Carey.

When Carey heard Jenny knocking at the front

screen, she was sorry she had been thoughtless. How much better it would have been if she had said she would go to Jenny's house. It was too bad that Mrs. Lee, busy with a new baby, had to stop doing what she was doing to bring Jenny over.

Jenny, however, was standing at the front door alone. Her white cane, held upright like a staff, came almost to her shoulder. Everything about her matched. Red socks, white shorts, red and white checked shirt. Carey wondered if her mother laid out the clothes she was to wear every morning.

"Did your mom bring you over?" asked Carey. Trying not to stare—she still could not quite believe that Jenny could not see—she focused on the top of her head.

"Nope," said Jenny. "I came by myself. Usually, though, when I go someplace new for the first time, someone goes with me. But this was easy. You see, I knew you lived next door and that the first sidewalk I came to would lead to your house."

Carey was impressed. *"I* couldn't do it," she said.

"You could if you had to," said Jenny. "But right now, what do you want to do?"

"Do?" said Carey doubtfully. Pudding was on her mind.

"I don't care. Go for a walk. Swing. Climb the tree in the side yard, play cards. Anything that's fun."

Carey did not know how to reply. All of the things Jenny had suggested they do sounded impossible. If they went for a walk, Jenny could fall down or get hit by a car. Walking from one house to another was simple compared to crossing streets. To get to Green Meadows Park, for instance, you had to cross Benton

Boulevard where there were no traffic lights. If they played on the monkey swing or climbed the apple tree, Jenny could fall and break her neck.

"Play cards," said Carey. It was the only thing Jenny had suggested they do where she could not hurt herself.

"I'll go home and get my special cards," said Jenny, "unless you want to come over to my house to play."

"Let's play here," said Carey. "I'll go over and get the cards for you."

"I'd better go by myself," said Jenny. "I might as well get the practice. I'll be going back and forth a lot, you know."

Jenny said that her special playing cards were printed in braille. To Carey, however, they looked like regular playing cards until Jenny pointed out the little bumps at the top and bottom of each card.

"Those little bumps tell you what card it is," said Jenny. "If the card is a jack of hearts, there will be the letter J and the letter H in braille. If it's the eight of hearts, it will have the H and number eight in braille. Do you understand?"

Carey said yes, though she had not the faintest idea what Jenny was talking about.

"Now this," said Jenny, picking up a card, "is the king of diamonds. Right?"

"Right," said Carey. Bumps or no bumps, she did not see how Jenny could tell.

"And this is the eight of diamonds."

"Right," said Carey.

"Of course, *you* don't have to pay any attention to the bumps. I'm just explaining it to you. Now what shall we play? Fish? Go Dig? King's Corners? I don't care.''

Carey knew how to play Fish and Go Dig but she did not know how to play King's Corners. So she said King's Corners. She thought this would give Jenny a little advantage.

"This is how you play it," said Jenny. She scooped up the deck of cards, shuffled them, and began dealing them out. Some went to her and some to Carey. The rest were placed in the middle, with one card turned face up. She felt it. "This is a clover. A ten."

"Club," said Carey. "A ten of clubs."

"I call them clovers," said Jenny, "because that's what they look like. Mama showed me the shape."

"Well, O.K.," said Carey. She would not argue with Jenny over a little thing like that. She could see and Jenny could not. And, of course, she would let Jenny win. Not by too much, because she might suspect something and that would make her mad.

"You can go first," said Jenny.

Carey said, "No, you."

"Well, then," said Jenny, "because this is a clover out here in the middle, if I have any clovers in my hand I can play them. Like this." With that, she took three cards from her hand, all clovers, and slapped them smartly down on the card in the middle. "Now, I draw one. And then, I have to throw one away." She sat back. "Your turn. Just remember, whoever gets rid of all her cards first, wins."

Carey's head was spinning. She had been so certain she would win the game she had not paid too close attention when Jenny explained it. But after thinking and thinking, she could only play one card. Then had to draw three more from the pile before she drew one she could use!

When she discarded one, Jenny reached out and felt the corner. "You shouldn't have thrown that one away," she said, kindly. "You have to remember which cards I played. You have to use your head. Now it's my turn again."

Jenny played two more cards in the middle and drew one from the pile. "If you're not careful," she said, "I'm going to win."

Carey was as careful as she knew how to be. At times, it looked as if Jenny were helping her. But even so, Carey kept getting more and more cards in her hand and Jenny had fewer and fewer until, at last, she had none at all.

"I win," said Jenny. "Do you want to play again?"

"Not right now," said Carey. "I have kind of a headache. Why don't we go for a little walk?"

Mrs. Lee had said it would be all right for Jenny to go for a walk with Carey. Carey had hoped it would not be.

Then, at the last moment, she was saved. They were just ready to start down the Lees' front steps when Carey saw the postman's little white truck coming down the street. Only it was not Mr. Mulligan who got out of the truck but Joannie Doane, who sometimes substituted for him.

Joannie, who had freckles and a ponytail, was wearing postman blue walking shorts. After leaving the

Lees' mail in their box, she again fished in the big brown leather bag and said, "Carey, your magazine has come at last. Do you want to take it or shall I leave it at your house with the other mail?"

"Oh, I'll take it!" cried Carey.

"I don't know what's been holding it up," said Joannie. "Probably it got stuck in Chicago. But never mind. It's a big, fat issue. There will be a lot of things for you and your friend to do. I took *Children's Fun* when I was about your age. I loved it."

How nice Joannie was, thought Carey, as the postgirl started back down the sidewalk. And what fun it would be, riding around in that little truck! She could be a postgirl when she grew up, if she wanted to. But Jenny . . . well, Jenny couldn't be anything at all. With this thought her mind raced ahead. Now that she had the magazine, what was she going to do with it? She and Debra had always read it together. Whoever read the fastest always politely waited for the other at the bottom of the page. But with Jenny? Carey's face began to burn. "I think I had better go home now, after all," she said.

"No!" cried Jenny. There was despair in her voice. "Don't go! Read me the magazine. Read me the contents, so we can see what we can do."

Carey reconsidered.

It was the first time Jenny had asked her to do anything. There was an expression on her face Carey had never seen before.

"Maybe I could stay a little longer," she said.

She sat down on the porch swing and began to read aloud. Joannie, the postgirl, had been right. The June

issue was full of things to do. The first thing listed in the contents was something called "The Hot Line."

"Read that," demanded Jenny. "Read about the hot line. It sounds like fun. Maybe we can do it."

The minute Carey started reading about the hot line, however, she began to worry. For her and Debra it would have been fine, but for her and Jenny . . . well, it would not work at all.

It went like this. Where two houses were next door to each other, the children could rig up a pulley arrangement so that a container—an empty coffee can would do nicely—could be relayed from one house to the other. The purpose of the can, of course, was to put messages inside so two friends could tell each other things in secret.

Jenny slapped her hands in excitement. "My father is very good at that sort of thing. He's a scientist, you know. He could do it."

"My father could do it, too, but . . ."

"Maybe they could do it together! We can send messages back and forth and we won't have to stick our heads out the window and yell."

"Except for one thing . . ." Carey said, her voice fading. She did not know how to continue.

"Except what? You mean, maybe your father wouldn't want a pulley thing coming out of his window?"

"Not that. It's just . . . well, we *can't* do it. Send messages, I mean. How can you see what I write? How can you see to write to me?"

Jenny laughed. A laugh that bubbled up like water from a drinking fountain. "Of course, I can't read your *writing*. And until I get my typewriter and learn to

35

type, the only thing I can write is my name. But not *seeing,* that isn't any problem. We'll both write in braille."

"B-braille," stuttered Carey. Even the thought of making words out of those tiny raised dots she had seen on the playing cards made her feel as if she had a fever. And to read them—well, she knew she couldn't do it, that was all.

"I think having a hot line is too young for us," said Carey. It was the most awful thing she could think to say.

"It's not!" insisted Jenny. "It can be our secret code. Even if that Pansy person finds something we've written, she won't be able to read it. And it's not hard to learn. Honest. It's fun. I started learning it when I was five."

"I really do have to go home," said Carey.

"Wait," said Jenny. "I'll get my slate and stylus and show you how easy it is."

Before Carey could say another word, Jenny had picked up her white cane and was on her way into the house.

Carey never wanted to hear the word *braille* again. She got to her feet and tried to walk. But something held her fast.

A minute later, Jenny came out of the house. "Carey?" she said. Her voice was small, questioning. "Carey, are you still here?"

Carey sighed inwardly. One more thing to put in the Bisness Book! Mentally, she wrote it down: "Always let a blind person know you're in the same room with them."

Aloud she said in a quite cross voice, "Of course I'm here. Where else."

"This is a slate," said Jenny. She put a metal object down on the porch table where she and Carey sat.

Carey picked it up. Hinged at one end, it was about eight or nine inches long and two inches high and had four rows of little "windows." How anybody could write anything with it, Carey did not know.

"And this is the stylus," continued Jenny. "You want to be careful and not hurt yourself."

Gingerly, Carey picked up a small spike stuck in a smooth wooden knob.

As Carey watched, Jenny took the slate and slipped a piece of paper inside. With the stylus in her right hand, she started making short little jabs across the slate.

"I'm making the braille alphabet for you to learn," said Jenny. "Are you watching?"

While Jenny was still demonstrating, Mrs. Lee came out on the porch. She was smiling. "I'm so glad you are going to learn braille," she said to Carey. "It will be fun for both you and Jenny. But you should have your own slate and stylus. You may have these to keep. And this is a braille alphabet card. It will help you, too."

Carey took the things Mrs. Lee handed her and said, "Thank you," but she was not thankful. She was not interested in raised dots. She did not want to learn to write braille. She did not want to learn to read it. What she wanted to do was go home and with her own eyes read the magazine that had caused all the trouble.

Jenny, however, was humming happily. "Oh, good!" she said. "Now, we can do it together. But first, I've got to tell you something."

Each one of the little windows in the slate, said Jenny, had six tiny grooves in it that the stylus fitted into. She said it was called a "cell." She showed Carey how, using the little grooves as a guide, you could punch six perfect little holes in the heavy paper, that came out as little bumps on the other side.

"Now, you do it," said Jenny.

Although Carey sighed as she leaned over the slate, punching those six little holes was easier than she thought it would be. When she turned her paper over, she found she had made six bumps that looked just like Jenny's.

Jenny felt them and nodded her approval. "Three bumps high and two bumps wide. Now, after I show you how to number them, I'll let you write something in braille."

Carey felt fresh alarm. She hated numbers. Math was the subject she liked least at school. She did not like Jenny saying "I'll let you." Whenever her father or Aunt Richard said they were going to "let" her do something, it usually was something she did not want to do.

But with Mrs. Lee looking out the window every now and then, she had no choice but to write the numbers Jenny gave her.

```
1 ● ● 4
2 ● ● 5
3 ● ● 6
```

But worse was to come.

"That's just the way you *read* braille," said Jenny, "from the bumpy side. When you write braille on your slate, you'll be punching the holes from the other side. That means the numbers will be turned around. The four, five, and six will be on the left and the one, two, and three on the right. Do you understand?"

"No," said Carey.

Jenny explained again.

Then, like a light going on, Carey got it! She turned her paper over, and on the side with the six little hollows, wrote down the numbers like this:

Even so, it wasn't easy. Each time Jenny called out a number, Carey had to look at her sample cell to see if she was doing it right. The fifth set of numbers—a one and a three and a four, five, six—was so hard Carey thought she couldn't go on.

Luckily, just then Jenny said, "You are through. Now let me see what you have written."

She ran her fingers lightly over the raised dots and her face shone. "You did it! But now, you look at it with your eyes and see if you can read it."

Carey looked:

But even with her sample cell and the alphabet card Mrs. Lee had given her, it took a few minutes to figure out what the raised dots spelled. Doubtfully, she said, "Carey. Does it spell Carey?"

Jenny beamed. "That's right! Of course, it doesn't have a big C for Carey, but I'll show you how to make capital letters later on. Now, look what I wrote for you."

As Carey took the paper, Aunt Richard's voice came floating across the side yards. "Car-eeeee! Come home, now! Time for lunch!"

Time for lunch? Carey could not believe it. Where had the morning gone? And she had thought she had been bored!

As soon as Carey finished her lunch, she went up to her room and shut the door. First, she read her name again in braille. Then, taking the alphabet card Mrs. Lee had given her, she began figuring out the row of raised dots on the paper Jenny had given her.

Tears rolled down Carey's cheeks as she wrote the proper letter under each group of dots.

I   M   GLAD   YOU

ARE   MY   FRIEND

She smudged away her tears. With a fresh piece of paper in the slate, the stylus in her hand, and the braille alphabet card before her, she began practicing her a, b, c's.

4

"Traveling"

Carey and her father walked over to the Lees' house that night after dinner. It was the first time the two fathers had met and it was the first time Carey had seen Mr. Lee up close. He was so tall, dark, and lean, and she thought he looked like Abraham Lincoln without his beard. Or his mole.

Mr. Lee, who was working on the motor of his car with Jenny helping, saw them coming. In a dark brown voice that matched his appearance, he said, "Jenny and I were planning on coming over to *your* house as soon as we finished our job here. I understand the girls have a job for us."

"That's right," Carey's father replied genially. "And I must say, I am more than happy to be living next door to a famous scientist. I understand you did some outstanding work on DNA."

Mr. Lee flapped a bony hand as if to wave any honor that had come to him away. "I just happened to be

41

doing the right thing at the right time. More important, have you met my daughter, Jenny?''

Carey's father said he had not had the pleasure. More introductions followed: Carey to Mr. Lee and Carey's father to Mrs. Lee, who had just come out on the porch with the baby.

Then, except for the baby, hands were shaken all around, both Mr. Lee's and Jenny's being rather greasy from working on the car.

Mr. Lee said, "Jenny has told me the principle of the hot line. The girls should have a lot of fun with it. It shouldn't be hard to install."

"Then we can do it?" said Jenny, jumping up and down like a jack-in-the-box.

"How soon, Daddy?" asked Carey. "Will it take long?"

Carey's father shook his head. "Not after we have the equipment on hand." He turned back to Mr. Lee. "This diagram in the magazine shows what we need."

Mr. Lee took the magazine, looked at the diagram.

"Hooks, pulleys, and a couple of hundred feet of good nylon rope should do it," said Carey's father. "I'll pick the stuff up in the next few days. There's a hardware store not too far from my office. The only problem is, I don't know how soon I'll be able to get to the job itself. I've a trip out of town coming up and some evening meetings scheduled. So it might be as late as the middle of next week, or even later, if that's all right with you."

"That suits me," said Jenny's father. "I'm working on a rather demanding project myself right now. But we'll manage to get together on it."

The two men shook hands and began chatting, while Jenny and Carey took turns pushing each other on the monkey swing.

As they swung, a corps of fireflies began flashing their little yellow taillights in among shrubs and flowers. Soon the fathers came around the corner of the house.

"Better come along now, Pumpkin," said Carey's father. "It's getting late."

"Bedtime for you, too," said Mr. Lee. "First, I'll give you a big push and then you can let the old cat die."

As good-byes were said all around, Carey tucked her hand inside her father's. Slowly, they walked across the dewy grass of the side yards toward home.

In a small voice Carey said, "I could see the fireflies. I could see the lights come on in all the houses. But Jenny didn't know it was getting dark."

"I know," said her father. "It's very sad."

"But *she* isn't sad," said Carey in a puzzled voice. *"I'm* the one."

"I know," said her father, after a short silence. "I shouldn't have said that. Blindness isn't sad unless a blind person, or even a person who can see, thinks it is. With a friend like Jenny, you'll get over being sad. One day, you'll never think about it at all."

The summer simmered on and still the fathers had not put up the hot line. First there was one reason and then another. The hardware store didn't have the kind of pulleys in stock that Carey's father wanted, and had to order them. There was a week of rain.

Then the fathers themselves were busy. Mr. Lee's research kept him late at the university. And Carey's father had a number of evening meetings with a client by the name of Sally Burns. Busy during the day with her own travel agency, the only time she could see about the settlement of her grandfather's large estate was after work at night.

Carey and Jenny, however, did not mind the delay. They were having fun.

Sometimes they played in Carey's room. Sometimes they played in Jenny's. In Carey's room, they took all the furniture in the dollhouse out and rearranged it. They pretended Paddington Bear and Miss Piggy had a romance. This was Carey's idea. She knew all about romances, her father having had several of them that, fortunately, had not worked out. They washed Miss Piggy's gown, a project that did not turn out well at all. It dried quite wrinkled, and Aunt Richard, who had to iron it afterward, became rather cross.

Carey liked Jenny's room better than her own. It had more interesting things in it.

"This, of course, is my bed," said Jenny, using it as if it were a trampoline. "And over there's my chest of drawers, my desk, and my chair."

Carey, who knew what these things were without being told, was poking around by herself.

"What's this?" she asked, picking up a strange-looking object on Jenny's desk. Made up of a lot of small round beads strung on wire, it looked like a baby's plaything.

"What's what?" asked Jenny, bouncing down from the bed and coming to stand by Carey.

"This thing." Carey put it in Jenny's outstretched hand.

"Oh, that's an abacus. I use it to work math."

Carey could have been no more surprised if Jenny said she used it to comb her hair.

"It's Chinese," said Jenny. "The Chinese use them all the time. It can do any kind of math there is."

Carey did not see how this was possible. All those little beads and wires do arithmetic! "Can it do like, well, like seventy-five times sixty-three?"

Jenny flipped some beads across the wires. "Four thousand, seven hundred, and twenty-five," she said. "Is that right? You can check it."

Carey did not know whether that was the right answer or not. She did not want to check it. She did not like math. And in particular, she did not like multiplication.

"Now give me a really hard one," said Jenny.

Carey pretended not to hear. She had moved on to a box sitting on one end of the desk.

That, Jenny explained in answer to Carey's question, was a talking book machine.

"A talking book machine!" repeated Carey. She had never heard of such a thing. But she was fascinated.

"All you have to do," said Jenny, "is look at the list they send you and pick out the book you want to read. Then you tell the people at the State Commission for the Blind and they send you the records. When you finish listening, you put the records in the case they came in and send them back. It doesn't cost anything. They even lend you the talking book machine."

Carey was fascinated all over again when Jenny told

her she "read" books on tape, too. The tapes also came from the Commission for the Blind. They also lent the machine to play them on if you didn't have one. Jenny, however, had her own.

"Daddy gave it to me for my birthday," said Jenny. "It's better than the kind they lend you. Theirs just plays. Mine records, too. Look, I'll show you how it works."

Jenny pushed the two buttons that made the machine record, then another that made it "play." She showed Carey how to "erase" what you'd recorded if you didn't want it any more, and how to speed the tape forward and backward.

Then they took turns pretending to be a famous lady television personality and interviewing each other on TV.

"Tell me, my dear," said Carey in an artificial voice, "and you must forgive me if I am asking an embarrassing question, but do you, ah, er, have difficulty eating? Being blind, that is."

"Not if I can find my plate," said Jenny in an equally silly manner. "But if someone has *hidden* it, that sometimes is a problem."

"And your meat; I am sure all our television audience would like to know how you handle meat."

"My moth-uh doesn't allow me to *handle* it. So messy, you know."

"But, my dear, I don't mean that kind of handle. How do you *cut* it?"

"With a knife," said Jenny.

They laughed so hard that Mrs. Lee, who was going down the hall, looked into Jenny's room to inquire what in the world was going on.

46

They played school. On her abacus, Jenny worked hard arithmetic problems Carey gave her. Jenny said she would work her arithmetic in real school the same way. She'd have to have some books in braille, of course, and a braille teacher who would show her "short ways" to write long words. This would help her to write and read braille faster. Mostly, though, she would do her schoolwork just like the other kids.

While Jenny worked her problems, Carey practiced braille. Without looking at the card Mrs. Lee gave her, she was able to write perfectly all the letters of the alphabet up to and including the letter N. She also knew R and Y because those letters were in her name.

Jenny made up sentences for her to practice on. This was not easy with ten letters of the alphabet still missing. But as Jenny said, most of the "good" letters came in the first half. "When you have to use a letter you don't know," said Jenny, "you can either look at the card or leave a space."

They played King's Corners. Sometimes Carey won. Sometimes Jenny did. They played on the monkey swing, pushing each other until their arches ached, and they climbed in the apple tree.

They made cookies at Jenny's house, taking turns with everything. Jenny confessed that the day they made the pudding, she had "showed off" a little. "Sometimes when people think I can't do something, I have to prove to them I can."

The next morning Aunt Richard said they could make cookies at Carey's house. But when she said it, she didn't know Jenny expected to do as much of the work as Carey.

47

Aunt Richard would not leave them alone. She was afraid Jenny would burn herself on the oven or get her fingers caught in the electric mixer. At last, Carey begged her to go away, saying they could manage very well. Aunt Richard then retreated as far as the doorway, clucking and offering advice and saying loud enough for them to hear, "I can't believe the child's mother allows her to do such things! If I'd had any idea that a blind child would actually be trying to *cook,* I would never have allowed them in the kitchen."

Finally, it was too much. Jenny went home in tears.

Jenny kept her room tidy because she had to. It would be hard for her to find things on her desk or in her closet. She never left anything sitting about on the floor or any drawers standing open.

So because Jenny kept everything in its proper place, Carey decided to keep her room tidy, too.

Finished with making her bed and putting her desk in order, Carey looked out her bedroom window just in time to see Jenny coming out her front door. She was wearing her white "carpenter" shorts, a dark blue T-shirt, and white socks with blue stripes. And, of course, carrying her long white cane.

Carey hurried downstairs.

"Hi," she said, remembering to speak first.

Jenny was smiling. "Guess what? Mom wants me to go on an errand—I mean, if you can go, too. Josh has a real bad rash on his bottom and needs this certain medicine. They have it at that drugstore in the shopping center. She called up to make sure. And I've got money, too, to buy us a double-decker cone!"

"I don't know if I can," said Carey. Even before

48

Jenny had finished speaking, she was thinking about all the hazards. First, they would have to cross Foster Avenue. Although there were traffic lights, it was a hard street to cross. Several blocks farther on, a big apartment building going up made walking difficult. A crew was busily tearing up the sidewalk. How would Jenny manage that? Carey felt a cold, hard lump in her stomach.

"I don't think I can go right now," Carey said, trying to sound sorry. "I'm pretty busy."

"Oh, please!" Jenny begged. "You have to. Mom won't let me go alone until I've been there quite a few times with someone. And Mom needs that medicine for Josh. Go ask your Aunt Richard if you can."

"I can't," said Carey. "She's not here." This was the truth, Aunt Richard having left a half hour before in her ancient Chrysler to do errands.

Jenny winked back tears.

Had she said no too quickly? Carey could not help wondering. She could not put off going for walks with Jenny forever. Before too long she would be responsible for seeing Jenny safely to school. "Perhaps if I left a note," said Carey, "Aunt Richard wouldn't care."

Mrs. Lee called, "Have a nice time!" as they started out, and Jenny caroled, "We will!" in return.

Carey, however, could not force herself to reply. She was thinking if it had been Aunt Richard waving them good-bye, she would have said, "Be careful," "Watch out for cars," or "Come straight home." Very likely she would have said all three.

But telling a person to be careful didn't help a bit. A person was careful because, well . . . she was careful because she *chose* to be.

49

Carey began to feel a sense of importance. The reason Mrs. Lee didn't warn them to be careful, she decided, was because of *her*. People would be watching as they passed them on the street. In her mind she could hear them say, "Isn't that sweet? That little girl helping that poor blind child. See how careful she is with her." "Yes," said another observer, "the blind child would have hurt herself seriously if it had not been for the alertness of that child with the curly braids."

This imaginary conversation was so real to Carey that in the time it took her to slow down and listen to it, Jenny was halfway to the corner. Moreover, she was walking along at so brisk a pace, her little white cane tracing quarter-arcs before her, that Carey had to run to catch up.

"Hey!" she yelled. "Wait! I'm coming!"

In a spurt, she caught up with Jenny and grabbed her arm a dozen paces from the corner. "Cars!" gasped Carey, the savior.

Jenny stopped so suddenly Carey had to apply brakes.

"I know there are cars," said Jenny. "I can hear them. And let go of my arm. Stop grabbing me."

"I'm not grabbing you," protested Carey. She was too surprised to have her feelings hurt. "I'm trying to *help* you."

"I know," said Jenny. "And I shouldn't have yelled at you. But it's better, you see, if I take *your* arm if I need to. That way we can go together." She tipped her head to one side like a robin listening for a worm. "The light is green now, isn't it, Carey? If it is, let's go."

Carey had been so busy looking out for Jenny that she had not paid any attention to the traffic lights. She looked up, and the light before her was green!

How could Jenny tell? Carey wished she knew. Curiously, however, even with her self-importance stripped away, Carey felt proud as Jenny hooked her left arm through Carey's right arm and they safely crossed the street.

Jenny, her arm still linked in friendly fashion through Carey's, managed the sidewalk where the new apartment was being built. Sometimes the tip of her white cane, sweeping from side to side, found an obstacle before Carey found it with her eyes. At times, it seemed the cane was an extension of her hand!

Even so, Carey felt enormous responsibilities. Jenny had already mentioned some of the things she wanted to be told about. Big holes in the sidewalk, for instance, that didn't have railings around them. Or curbings that had been pared down so it was sometimes hard to tell where the sidewalk stopped and the street began. Also, she would like to hear about interesting things that happened as they passed by. And people. Most of all she liked to hear about people.

Once again, Carey began to swell with importance. The drugstore where they were going was large. Jenny would need help finding the baby ointment department. Paying for it would be a problem. And how would she pay for the treat they were to have before starting home?

As the electric-eye door to the drugstore opened, Jenny stopped and took a big sniff. "It's big!" she said. "So many different smells!"

Carey took a big sniff. The store did indeed smell

big. There were smells of candy, perfume, popcorn, and people, as well as some other smells. She looked around. Here and there signs, hung from the ceiling, told where things could be found. But nowhere did she see a sign saying Medicine.

"I guess we'll have to ask where the medicine department is," said Carey.

Before Jenny finished answering, however, a clerk wearing a white jacket and a worried expression came hurrying toward them. "Is your little friend looking for something?" he said to Carey.

Carey stared at him owlishly. She felt angry. "Ask her," she said. "She's not deaf. Ask her."

"Ask her?" repeated the clerk, sputtering. "Oh, yes. I see. Pardon me." Then in a loud voice said, "May I help you, Miss?"

"I would like a large tube of Diapure Ointment," said Jenny.

"Diapure Ointment," said the clerk. "Follow me."

At the counter to which he led them, the clerk took a box from the shelf behind him, slipped it into a small sack, and stapled it shut. "That will be one dollar and seventy-three cents, including tax." Careful to look neither at Jenny nor Carey, he focused his eyes somewhere between them.

Carey moved in a little closer, ready to take over. But already Jenny was taking a small red billfold from her white canvas shoulder bag. Then, from the billfold, she took out two one-dollar bills and laid them on the counter.

"One seventy-three from two dollars," said the clerk, ringing the cash register. "And here's your change. One seventy-five, one eighty, one ninety, and

53

two." Carefully, one by one, he fed the coins into the palm of Jenny's left hand.

Although another customer had arrived at the counter, the clerk made no move to help her until Jenny had felt each coin and put them in her billfold.

As they moved away from the counter, their dignity collapsed. For the clerk's "Have a nice day!" had been followed by a quite distinct "Phew!" of relief.

With the Diapure Ointment tucked away in Jenny's shoulder bag, the girls walked down the street to Bobbit's ice cream store. Some shoppers made way for them, moving to the outer edge of the sidewalk. One man Carey did not like at all. Before he shuffled on, she noticed he had a peaky gray face that matched the shabby suit he wore. Although Carey hoped Jenny could not "feel" such people staring, she rather enjoyed it. Several times she thought she heard passers-by comment on their progress. She also enjoyed telling Jenny, who had not been to this shopping center before, about all the different shops they passed. Her favorite, she said, was the ice cream store. Jenny would love it. It had a pink and white candy-striped awning out in front. And Bobbit's really *was* an ice cream store. The only things it sold other than ice cream were magazines, newspapers, and greeting cards. These were up near the entrance. All the rest was ice cream. It cost more than it did at other places, but it was worth it. Mr. and Mrs. Bobbit made it themselves.

"You see," she said, "they've got this big glass case. You walk along it and pick out the kind of ice cream you want. Then, the lady behind the counter either makes it into a cone for you or she packs it in pints or quarts. If you want, she will put it in a dish and you can sit at one of the little tables in the back of the room and eat it."

"Mmmmmm," said Jenny. "I can't wait."

"You don't have to wait," said Carey. "Here we are."

5

The Face on the Magazine Cover

The names of all fifty different kinds of ice cream were listed on a large sign on the wall. Carey read them to Jenny, starting with Apple Nut Crispy Crunch and ending with Youngberry Yummy Delight.

"So far, I've had eighteen different kinds," said Carey. "So it's getting harder and harder to make up my mind. My ambition is to have all fifty."

Jenny said it was her ambition to have all fifty, too, but it would take her a little while to catch up.

After much choosing and rejecting—during which time Carey read aloud the names of all the fifty varieties once again—Carey finally settled on Marshmallow Nut Fudge and Jenny on Karmel Krunch Pecan.

Meanwhile, some other customers who knew exactly what they wanted came in, so Carey and Jenny had to wait a bit longer. Presently the clerk came up to them. She was short and fat—in fact, she was shaped rather like a cone—and had a big pile of pinkish hair done up in a hairnet. She looked first at Jenny and made a sympathy sound. Then she turned to Carey. "All right, my dear," she said. "And what will it be for you today?"

"Marshmallow Nut Fudge," said Carey, "in a double-decker cone."

"And your little friend, here?" She tossed her mound of hair in Jenny's direction. "What will *she* have?"

Carey began to feel hot all over. She'd felt that way when the drugstore clerk had acted as if Jenny, as well as being blind, could neither hear nor speak. It wasn't fair!

"Don't ask me," she said, giving the clerk her owly-scowly look. "Ask *her.*"

"What did you say?" The woman cast an uneasy look at Jenny, who had turned a bright salmon pink.

"She's not *deaf,*" said Carey. "She can *hear.* She can *talk.* Ask her."

"Oh," mumbled the clerk. "I didn't mean anything. It's just that . . . I thought . . ."

"I'll have a Karmel Krunch Pecan double-decker cone, if you please," said Jenny, who could be quite nice when she chose.

"A Karmel Krunch Pecan and a Marshmallow Nut Fudge," said the clerk. Glad to be busy, she began packing two rather larger than usual scoops of ice cream into cones that were a Bobbit's speciality. They were a dark, crusty brown and printed all over with a design of little squares.

"Pay the cashier, please," said the clerk. She then added in a voice just above a whisper, "Will your little friend be able to handle the cone by herself?"

"Try me and see," said Jenny. "Give it to me."

With that, Jenny stuck out her tongue and with one swift circular lick, followed by a large bite, reduced the top of the cone by almost half!

Carey laughed. She could not help it.

Then the woman behind the counter laughed so hard she had to take a piece of tissue from the pocket of her uniform and wipe her eyes. "I deserved that," she said.

Giggling, just as they had in the drugstore, the girls made their way to the cashier's desk at the front of the store. "I expect you'll have to hold my cone while I pay the bill," said Jenny, still laughing. "Just don't let *her* see you do it."

Holding both cones, but being very careful to lick only from her own, Carey watched as Jenny skipped over a one-dollar bill and took out a five-dollar bill.

"Here's a five," she said, as she put it down on the counter. "And here's our check for two double-decker cones."

Showing no surprise, the cashier gave Jenny three one-dollar bills and the correct change in return. "I've a nephew who is blind and I've noticed he folds his five-dollar bills the long way, just as you do. The one-dollar bills he leaves just as they are, and the tens he folds in half the other way."

"I've not had any ten-dollar bills yet," said Jenny, "but when I do, that is the way I'll fold mine."

So that was the way Jenny told the difference between one-dollar bills and five-dollar bills! It was easy, once you thought about it. And no doubt there was an easy though a different way to tell nickels from quarters and dimes from pennies. And how to choose socks to match the clothes she was wearing. There were probably dozens and dozens of other things blind people had a different way of doing. A way that was just as good.

Such practical matters, however, were driven from her mind as her eyes fell on a stack of magazines piled on the floor near the door. Evidently they had just been delivered, for they were still tied with stout brown cord. The cord, however, and a strip of wrapping paper could not conceal the face on the cover.

"Hey!" said Carey. "Wait a minute. I want to look at something."

Leaving Jenny, who was standing near the door, she turned back to the pile of magazines. Bending closer, she could see that, without any doubt, it was the dark, handsome face of Mr. Lee looking back at her!

"Hey!" said Carey again. She could not keep the excitement from her voice. "Come here. Your dad's picture is on the cover of this magazine."

"My dad?" said Jenny. "What magazine?"

"It's called *Newsmakers, The Magazine of Important People,"* said Carey. "And it's your dad, all right. Beside his picture it says in big letters, 'Rich man's son seeks sci, scientific see-clusion.' Do you know what that means?"

"Well," said Jenny, who had moved to Carey's side. "It means he just wants to be a biologist and do research on DNA and not do all the business things Grandpa Lee wants him to do."

Carey understood what Jenny meant but she wanted to know more. "If it didn't cost a dollar and fifty cents, we could buy a copy," she said, thinking of the money in the little red billfold.

"I've got money," said Jenny, "but it's Mama's. I wouldn't want to spend it unless she told me to." She hesitated. "I suppose I could spend it, if I paid her back from my allowance."

"Better not do that, my dear," said a nearby voice.

Carey looked around. The man who had spoken wore a seersucker suit from which grubby shirt sleeves hung out. He had thin gray hair and a complexion Aunt Richard would quite definitely call "peaky." He had a familiar look.

"But I believe *I'll* buy a copy," said the gray man in a silky voice. He crouched beside the pile of magazines. The blade of a penknife flashed in his soft white hands as he cut the cord that bound them. He took a magazine from the top of the pile and got rather nimbly to his feet.

"You will pardon me," he said, "but I could not help but overhear part of your conversation. The gentleman whose picture is on the cover of the magazine is the father of this young lady?" He tipped his head toward Jenny.

Carey could have given the same tart reply to the stranger she gave to the drugstore clerk and the ice cream lady. Twice in one day, however, was enough. Besides, the stranger *was* a stranger and it seemed impolite not to answer a simple question.

"Yes," she said.

Jenny tugged at Carey's arm. "We'd better go now," she said, "or Mama is going to start to worry."

Walking home, Carey said, "You know the man who talked to us in the ice cream store?"

Jenny nodded. "I didn't like him much. He chewed gum, too. Juicy Fruit."

Carey laughed. Now that Jenny mentioned it, she remembered she'd smelled it, too.

"And he limps a little," added Jenny. "He shuffled. He was right behind us when we left the store."

As Carey, ready to say, "Well, he's not following us now," turned around to look, a van came around the corner. It was a dark, dirty green. The sign once painted on its side was now unreadable. At the wheel of the van was the man with the gray face and the shabby suit. He was staring straight ahead.

Carey was about to mention this interesting fact to Jenny when another car came tootling around the corner. This time it was Aunt Richard in her ancient Chrysler.

In about a second she had hustled the girls in the car. There she began a safety lecture that lasted all the way home.

"You could have knocked me over with a feather," Aunt Richard said at dinner that night. "I turned the corner onto Forty-second Street, and there they were!"

"But they were all right?" asked Carey's father, looking up from a brussels sprout he had been trying to spear with his fork.

"Of course they were all right," said Aunt Richard crisply. Her nose turned pink as it always did when she was nervous or excited. "But they might *not* have been. They'd already crossed Foster Avenue, which is a positive menace. And there's a great, yawning hole in front of that new apartment building that's going up. Jenny might have fallen in, dragging Carey after her."

"But she didn't?" said Carey's father. "They didn't—fall in, I mean?"

Carey knew her father was teasing Aunt Richard. She knew, too, that presently Aunt Richard would say she knew she was nothing but an old fussbudget. Her father would then say, "Oh, no you're not! I never could have raised Carey without you." And then everything would be peaceful again.

Even though Carey was certain this was the turn the conversation would take, it did not seem to be a good time to bring up seeing Mr. Lee's picture on the cover of the magazine. And she could scarcely do that without bringing up the stranger she had talked to. Any talk of strangers would only give Aunt Richard one more thing to worry about.

That night before Carey went to bed, she made a new entry in the Bisness Book:

Don't take there arm. They do not like it. Let them take your arm, above the elbow.

Although the girls had been discussing it for some time, Carey waited until Aunt Richard had time to get over their walk to the shopping center before asking if Jenny could spend the night.

Even then, the answer was a firm no.

"I couldn't take the responsibility," said Aunt Richard. "The poor child might get up in the night and fall downstairs."

"But she wouldn't!" cried Carey. "She's very careful. She doesn't fall down any more than I do."

"I'm sorry, Carey. I like Jenny. She is a remarkable little girl. But you must remember this is not her house. She does not know it like she knows her own. If anything should happen to her while she was under this roof, I would never forgive myself."

Carey wanted to tell Aunt Richard she'd had other mistaken notions about blind people. One of her mistakes was about them being "musical." She remembered her saying that right after the Lees moved in. Some were musical. Some were not. Jenny wasn't musical at all. The piano belonged to Mrs. Lee, and both she and Jenny's father played it very well. Another thing. Jenny's parents did not like people to call her "remarkable." They said any blind child of normal intelligence, given the proper training, could do as well.

But with Aunt Richard in a mood like this, Carey knew it would do no good to argue. "Well, then," she said, "can I spend the night with Jenny? Daddy told me at breakfast he won't be home tonight. He has a meeting with Miss Sally Burns."

Aunt Richard made wrinkles run across her forehead. "Have you been invited? Did Jenny's mother say it was all right with her?"

Carey nodded, though matters had not yet gone this far.

"In that case, I suppose you may," said Aunt Richard. "But don't forget the first time you stayed all night with Debra Denman. You got so homesick I had to go over to her house at midnight and bring you home."

"But Aunt Richard!" Carey was outraged. "Then I was only six! After that, I spent the night with Debra Denman about a thousand times!"

"Scarcely that," said Aunt Richard, dryly. "Now you run along and play—and no walks, do you hear? I'm going to take the car and run down to Mr. Thrush's market to see if his fresh rhubarb is in."

Staying all night with Jenny was as much fun as it had been with Debra, Carey decided. After the baby was in bed, they all played King's Corners. Mrs. Lee made popcorn and they drank soda and played until past their bedtime.

When they went upstairs, the girls put on their pajamas. Jenny hopped into bed but after Carey put out the light she stared out the window at her own house.

It was not surprising her own room was dark, nor Aunt Richard's. Aunt Richard went to bed right after the ten o'clock news. But her father's room was dark, too. He was having a long meeting with Sally Burns.

Carey got back in bed beside Jenny, who was crocheting a dish cloth out of string.

"I'm sick," said Carey. "I think I may throw up."

"You're not sick," said Jenny practically, from the darkness. "You're jealous."

"Am I?" asked Carey.

She was surprised.

"Of course, being jealous *is* a kind of sickness," Jenny admitted, "only you don't have a fever. I had it when Josh was born because I thought Mama and Daddy would like him better than they did me. But they didn't, really. They paid more attention to him

64

because he was new. And also because he was a boy. Now, I know they like us both the same."

"But Sally Burns isn't a baby," argued Carey. "She's a grown person and my father likes her a lot."

"But do you like her?" asked Jenny.

"I don't know," said Carey doubtfully. "I've only seen her once. Since then, I keep wondering what would happen if she and my father got married. If they did, my Aunt Richard might go away and I wouldn't know what to do."

"But maybe your Aunt Richard wouldn't go away. Sally Burns works, doesn't she, at her travel agency? Maybe your Aunt Richard would stay and keep house for you. Then you would have both of them."

While Carey was thinking this over, Jenny went to sleep.

Carey soon dropped off to sleep herself. Therefore, she did not know how late it was when her father came home from his business meeting with Sally Burns, which was just as well.

6

The Good Word Gets Around

Carey did not know how the word got around. Dozens of kids she had never seen before, plus a few parents, turned up the morning the two fathers finally prepared to put up the "hot line."

A number of cars slowed or paused as they passed the house, their owners curious as to what was going on, as did a dirty green van with faded lettering on its side.

Aunt Richard, arms folded, watched from the porch.

In the front row of spectators in the side yard was Pansy Prugh. She was wearing a tattered white tutu over a skimpy red bathing suit. "Look at my tan," she demanded. "I am tan-der than anyone here. That is because I have been to Lake Michigan."

No one, however, looked at Pansy. Everyone was looking at the fathers and the equipment for the "hot line" that was spread out on the grass.

Without a trace of a smile Carey's father said, "Jack, if you have no objection, why don't I go ahead and install the hooks and the pulleys outside the girls' windows, and you see to stretching the rope between them."

"Why, Tom," said Mr. Lee, his face every bit as serious as Carey's father's, "that's very nice of you, but I thought I'd put up the hooks and the pulleys and leave the business of the rope to you."

Suddenly, one of the bigger boys among the spectators laughed. "I get it," he shouted. "Unless somebody's got a tall ladder, how are you planning to get the rope stretched between those two upstairs windows?"

"Easy!" offered another voice. "Just tie one end of the rope to a rock and throw it over."

"Throw a rock all that distance and not break a window or hurt somebody? You're crazy. The way to do it is to tie one end of the rope to an arrow and shoot it over."

"Fasten one end of the rope to a fishing pole and just hand it up!"

After that, suggestions grew sillier and sillier and laughter louder and louder, until Aunt Richard came to the rescue.

"What in the world is all this commotion about?" she said, in her most commanding voice. "Getting a loose end of rope up there, however you go about it, won't do you any good. First of all, you've got to loop the rope around one of the pulleys and splice the ends. If you happen to have a couple of U-clamps, that would do very nicely."

"We have them," said Carey's father.

"Well, then," said Aunt Richard approvingly, "the job's half done. The next step is to drop a nice long piece of cord out of the other window, tie it to your pulley rope, and haul it up."

Carey's father immediately declared Aunt Richard was a genius.

Jenny's father said Aunt Richard has missed her calling. He said she could get a job in the physics department of the university any day.

Carey, however, suspected that both fathers might have had the same idea as Aunt Richard all along.

Most of the spectators, however, did not catch on until the operation was completed.

When Carey and Jenny each appeared in her own bedroom window, loud cheers arose.

Carey rang Aunt Richard's dinner bell, which had been lent for the occasion. Calling across to Jenny, she said, "Are you ready?"

"Ready!" answered Jenny. "I'm starting to pull!"

A minute later the coffee can, with Carey's braille message inside, went bobbling across the side yards, high above the heads of the spectators.

Carey waited nervously. She had put a lot of thought into her message for Jenny. She had also taken a lot of pains writing it in braille. She hoped she had made no mistakes. That would not be fair.

A few minutes later when Jenny, from her window, rang a dinner bell and cried, "Are you ready?" Carey's heart began to beat a little faster.

"Ready!" she yelled. "I'm starting to pull."

Then, just as it was supposed to do, the coffee can came bobbling back across the way.

As Carey read Jenny's message, a shrill voice rose from down below.

It belonged, unmistakably, to Pansy Prugh. "What did you write to Jenny, Carey? If she can't see, how could she read it? If Jenny can't see, how can she write to you?"

Carey considered. She did not want to share her and Jenny's first messages on the hot line with anyone. But still . . .

Only the night before, her father had told her a story about Alexander Graham Bell. For a long time he had been working on a new invention. It was to be called a "telephone." However, he had never tested it until one night, alone in his laboratory, a beaker of acid upset. Badly burned and needing help, he decided to call his friend Dr. Watson. Desperately, he spoke into the mouthpiece of his invention. "Dr. Watson," he said. "Come here. I need you." And at the other end of the wire, Dr. Watson heard. And came! As a result, Alexander Graham Bell lived to become famous and his words, "Dr. Watson, come here. I need you," were printed in all the history books.

Someday, Carey thought, her message to Jenny might become famous, too, and would be printed in all the history books. In the meantime, however, it hardly seemed fair to keep it to herself. Leaning out the window, she yelled in a voice loud enough for Pansy Prugh and all the rest of the world to hear, "IT'S O.K. TO BE BLIND!" Then she drew in her head.

She was not so sure about the famousness of Jenny's message to her. Jenny had written, "Come over." Carey decided that was not worth another yell.

*   *   *

For the next few weeks there was so much dinging and a-linging from the silver dinner bell that Carey used to summon Jenny to the hot line, Aunt Richard declared it gave her a headache.

She also complained that whenever she awakened in the night, she heard punching noises coming from Carey's bedroom. She said the first thing Carey's father knew, the child would not only be writing everything in braille, she would blindfold herself and be walking with one of those long white canes.

That, indeed, is exactly what Carey *was* thinking the morning she traced Aunt Richard to the kitchen.

"I'm going over to Jenny's house," Carey said. "O.K.?"

Aunt Richard, who had got a bargain in strawberries the day before at Mr. Thrush's market, turned from the kettleful of preserves simmering on the stove. "For a little while. Don't get in Mrs. Lee's way, and be home by noon."

With an "I will" tossed over her shoulder, Carey sped across the side yards.

Josh, the baby, was wide awake in his buggy on the shady porch. Carey stopped to look at him. He was twice as big as when the Lees moved in. She had not known a baby could grow so fast. She noticed also, he had turned from his stomach—which was the way Mrs. Lee always put him down to sleep—to his back. It was his latest trick. He could also do something even more exciting. He had learned to smile! As Carey leaned over the buggy and touched his chin with her forefinger, the corners of his little mouth turned up and at the same time he made a happy-baby sound that was like the cooing of doves.

Carey cooed back at the baby. She held up a rattle she had found in the buggy and his little hands, shaped like tiny starfish, reached out to try and touch it.

Once, when Jenny was away from home on an errand with her father, Mrs. Lee had told Carey that Jenny had only been a little older than Josh when they discovered she couldn't see. "At first," she said, "I'm afraid we panicked. Then we learned from a very wise man—blind himself and a teacher—that blindness isn't the tragedy most people think it is. That at most it is a nuisance. We learned that Jenny, with proper training and the proper attitude on our part, would be able to do almost everything other children do. And that's exactly the way it has worked out! Now, we know that when Jenny grows up, she can be anything she wants to be. A teacher, a computer programmer, a lawyer, an engineer . . . whatever she wants to be, she'll find a way."

As Carey was remembering all that Mrs. Lee had said, Jenny came out on the porch. "Mama said you were here. She saw you through the window talking to the baby. Did you come to play?"

Suddenly, Carey did not want to tell Jenny why she had come over. Later, perhaps, she would ask Jenny to show her how to use the long white cane. Maybe later, much later, she would become a "travel teacher" like the person who had taught Jenny to go everywhere.

"I came to play," she said.

"Edna," said Carey's father at dinner a few nights later. "Are you trying to make a vegetarian out of me?"

71

Aunt Richard's nose turned pink and her lips clamped shut as tightly as if they had been fastened with a clothespin. She did not like to be called Edna. In fact, she hated it. When someone called her that, as Carey's father sometimes did to tease her, she would not reply.

"Very well, then," said Carey's father to the silence. "Miss Richard, are you trying to make a vegetarian out of me?" He looked down at his plate. "Not that I mind, you understand. But here before me, I see fresh green beans, carrot and celery sticks, and creamed cauliflower. And on my salad plate, I have lettuce, tomatoes, cucumbers, parsley, and yes, a bit of green pepper."

"But fresh vegetables are in season," said Aunt Richard, as the pinkness of her nose began to fade. "And you cannot very well be a vegetarian when you have two pieces of fried chicken on your plate."

"Chicken!" exclaimed Carey's father. "In the presence of all these wonderful fresh vegetables, I quite overlooked the chicken." He took a bite. "Delicious! But then everything is well prepared, as usual."

Though Aunt Richard sniffed, she looked pleased. "I can read you like a book, Thomas Cramer. After having your fun teasing me, you are now trying to butter me up."

"Sally Burns is very fond of vegetables. If she came to dinner some night, do you think we might have this very same meal?"

Aunt Richard's nose turned pink again. "I suppose we *could*." She looked at the food on the table as if she had never seen it before. "Though it might be nicer if, instead of the creamed cauliflower, we had asparagus with hollandaise. Mr. Thrush's asparagus was very nice when I was there yesterday. For dessert we could have a nice green-apple pie."

Jenny clambered down from a branch of the apple tree where she and Carey had been sitting.

"I want to run," said Jenny.

Carey said, "What?" though she had heard perfectly what Jenny said.

"My legs want to run," said Jenny. "They get tired of just walking around."

"Where do you want to do it?" Carey said cautiously.

"I don't care. Someplace where I won't bump into a lot of things. The school playground, maybe. Though on playgrounds, if you fall down you skin your knees. A park would be best. It would be nice to run on grass."

Carey thought. She liked to run, too. She had been the best runner among the fourth-grade girls.

"Green Meadows Park would be perfect," said Carey. "It's the other way from the plaza where we went to get the medicine for Josh. And it's not too far. Besides, we go right past Clarkson School and I can show you where you're going to go this fall."

"I'll ask Mom if we can go," said Jenny, heading for the house.

"And I'll ask Aunt Richard," said Carey, climbing down from the tree.

Aunt Richard, however, was not enthusiastic. "I don't like you taking the responsibility," she said, "though if Jenny's mother says yes, I don't see what business it is of mine."

"Her mother already did say yes," said Carey. "I can see Jenny through the window. She's in front of our house right now, waiting to go."

"Well," said Aunt Richard, thinking aloud as she sometimes did, "two children, together, even if one of them is blind, should be safe enough. But don't talk to anyone you meet along the way. Watch out at all the intersections. Stay on the playground where there's supervision. Don't go wandering around all over the park."

"I won't," said Carey. "I mean I will. I'll do everything you say."

She was halfway to the door when Aunt Richard called her back. "On your way home you might stop at Mr. Thrush's market and buy me a nice green pepper. It's scarcely a block out of your way. You can tell Mr. Thrush I'll be in Saturday to settle my account. And if he'd pick the pepper out himself, tell him I would be much obliged."

"I've got to be back at four o'clock for sure," said Jenny. "So I thought I'd better wear my watch."

"Watch?" said Carey politely. By now she knew better than to be surprised at anything Jenny might say or do.

"It's a braille watch," said Jenny, holding out her arm. "When you want to know what time it is, you press the winder and it opens up like this." She pressed the winder and the crystal covering the watch flew up. "See? It's got bumps as well as numbers. It's as easy as pie to tell the time."

With Jenny lightly holding her arm, they started out. Now that she knew how to walk with Jenny, Carey liked doing it. She liked describing the different things she saw.

There was a bright pink house with green shutters and a wooden cut-out of a Dutch girl with a watering can watering wooden tulips. They met a funny-looking dog, as long and as low as a dachshund, covered with fur like a cocker spaniel. And there was Clarkson School, where both of them would go that fall. They walked all the way around it, with Carey telling Jenny where the principal's office was and where the different rooms were located.

Carey particularly liked pointing out anything that might cause Jenny trouble. For instance, a curbing that had been cut down. That was good for people in wheelchairs but not so good for blind people, who sometimes couldn't tell when they were stepping from the sidewalk into a busy street.

Jenny liked asking questions, too. Carey liked answering them, if she could.

How big was Riverville, Jenny wanted to know. How many people?

Carey had no idea, though she did not like to admit it. "It's bigger in the winter when all the kids going to college are here. In the summer, a lot of them go home."

"Anyway," said Jenny, taking a big sniff. "I like it better than a really big city. I mean, like New York."

"I didn't know you'd lived *there*," said Carey respectfully. "I went there once with Daddy. To a meeting."

"Of all the places we've lived," said Jenny, "I think I am going to like it here best of all. I can go everywhere."

"Maybe you can't go *everywhere*," said Carey. "The other half of Riverville, the part that's on the other side of the river, isn't very nice. It 'died,' my father says, because it didn't get any nourishment. The railroad stopped coming through. And now there's just these big old warehouses and buildings and rusty tracks that no one uses any more. The people who lived and worked there once have all moved away."

"Ugh!" said Jenny. "Then that's O.K. I wouldn't want to go there anyway."

But the park, they agreed, was nice. Carey described it. There was something there for everybody. A shelterhouse to use for picnics when it rained. A rose garden, tennis courts, a woods to walk in, and a playground for little kids. A little farther on and next to the woods was a big grassy field where bigger kids threw Frisbees, played ball, or did anything they wanted to do.

Carey had hoped they would have the grassy area all to themselves. However, when they reached the crown of a little hill, Carey could see that a man and a bunch of kids were already there. They seemed to be running, too.

"Will there be room for us to run, too?" asked Jenny.

"Lots," said Carey. "All we have to do is go over to the other side."

Tall trees backed up to the place Carey had chosen as their starting place. The man and the children were at least a half block away.

Jenny put down her cane. "Can I run now? Tell me what direction. And tell me when to stop."

Carey looked doubtful. "Maybe we'd better run together. We could hold hands and run side by side."

Jenny's chin jutted out the way it did the day they had first met. "It won't be any fun unless I run by myself."

"Well, then, O.K.," said Carey, still doubtful. "Just wait until I go over there a way. Then, when I yell, you can run in my direction. And when I yell again, that means it's time to stop."

Carey ran to a point halfway between the place Jenny waited and the man and the children were gathered. "Here I am!" she called. "And don't forget your cane!"

"I don't use my cane when I run," Jenny called. "Here I come!"

Carey felt almost envious. She had not known Jenny could run so fast. Her face was lifted to the sun she could feel but could not see. The wind was combing her hair with its fingers.

Then, for a moment, Carey's heart stood quite still. Jenny was no longer running toward her but had veered off in the direction of the man and the children.

"This way, Jenny! This way!" Carey called. "Over here. Here I am!"

But if Jenny heard, she gave no sign.

"Stop, Jenny! Stop!"

After that, there was nothing she could do. She shut her eyes to blot out the sight.

The speeding Jenny had run into the gathering of children and scattered them like leaves before a high wind.

7

Where Is Jenny?

Jenny would be embarrassed. Jenny would be crying. *At least I would be crying,* thought Carey, *if I were in her place.* Without her long white cane in a strange place, Jenny would be lost.

Carey picked the cane up from the high green grass and, half walking and half running, started off across the field. Although she was still too far away to see what was going on, she could tell that the little group had somehow rearranged itself.

As she drew closer, one thing became quite clear. Jenny was not crying. Seated on the grass, tailor-fashion, she was laughing! The man with the cut-off jeans and white T-shirt was laughing too. Around them the children, politely curious, were gathered. Some of them, Carey thought, were about her age. Others a little older.

The man looked up when he saw Carey coming. "Hi, there!" he called. "Jenny told me you'd be along." As he walked toward Carey in greeting, she thought she had never seen anyone so big and strong. Nor anyone whose hair was so copper-red and curly. "My name is Adam," he said. "And these are my kids. Not my *own* kids—though I've got one on the way—but my kids nonetheless." He waved a deeply tanned muscular arm toward the youngsters. "Pete, Carlos, Maria, Booker, Linda, and Walter."

"Hi," said Carey. In the midst of so many new faces, black and white and brown, she felt shy.

"Hi!" the children caroled.

Jenny called out, "Did you bring my cane?"

"What you don't know about these kids," Adam said to Carey, "is that some of them may, one day, be going to the Olympics." He grinned. "That may be a slight exaggeration, but who knows? In the meantime, I'm helping them train for the kid's intercity track meet next spring. I had good entries for both boys and girls in the low hurdles and the four-forty, but what I needed was a sprinter. Then look who came running straight into me!"

"I did!" screamed Jenny, jumping up and down. "I ran smack into him. I was coming so fast I almost knocked him down!"

"Man, did she ever!" said a boy, whose T-shirt said his name was Walter. "She was running about a hundred miles an hour."

"But nobody got hurt," said a black girl with tiny braids wrapped neatly around her head. "Adam caught her just in time or she might have fallen down."

"No, I wouldn't have!" said Jenny hotly. "Besides, Adam says I'm a natural."

"A natural what?" asked Carey. With "Adam this"

and "Adam that" and Jenny acting not like herself at all, she didn't know what was going on.

"I said that Jenny seems to be a natural runner," said Adam. "All these kids here are naturals. They've got the right build for it, but more important, they want to run. You see, I'm a junior-high track coach. Although my school makes me teach phys ed, too, my first love is track. So, during the summer vacation I scout around for good runners and give them a few pointers."

"And that's not all, either!" Jenny put in excitedly. "That track meet next spring, well, Adam says maybe I can be in it!"

"That's right," said Adam. "The problem will be to figure out a way to keep Jenny in the proper lane while she runs. I've an idea, if I can work it out. And of course, I'll have to check with the officials of the track meet. They may not like one of the runners wearing something on her head like a girl from Mars."

"What's your idea?" asked the boy Adam had called Carlos.

"I can't say for sure. I'm going to have to pick the brains of a fella I know who works at the telephone company. He's an electrical wizard. A blind wizard, as a matter of fact. To hear him tell it, though, he's just an ordinary guy. I'll let you know after I talk to him. In the meantime, I want you kids to run every day and keep our training rules. Plenty of sleep. Easy on the junk food: french fries, candy bars, and soda pop. I don't want you clogging up your arteries with fat before you reach the age of fifteen." He glanced at his watch. "Well, it's time to break this up for today. See you all same time, same place next week. And if

81

you've any friends who are runners, bring them along.
O.K.?"

"O.K., Adam! See ya!" sang a chorus of voices.

As the children scattered, Adam turned to Jenny.
"If this thing I have in mind works out, I'll call your
parents, just to be sure it's all right with them."

"Oh, it will be!" said Jenny. "They'll let me tackle
anything."

"I believe you're right," Adam laughed. "But I'd
still like to check with them anyway." He took a stub
of pencil and a small notebook from the back pocket of
his cut-offs. "If you'll tell me your father's name."

"Lee," said Jenny. "His first name is John, though
he likes it better if you call him Jack. His middle name
is Talbert but he keeps that a secret if he can."

"Oh, *that* Lee," said Adam, with a thoughtful look.

"My mother's name is Lucy and her middle name
is—"

"Your father's name will be enough," said Adam,
suddenly brisk. "I'd like to get the name of your
friend, however."

"Oh," said Jenny, with an offhand air. "That's
Carey. She lives next door to me."

"Carey, I'm glad to meet you," said Adam. "Do
you also like to run?"

Carey nodded. Until Adam spoke directly to her,
she had felt herself growing smaller and smaller, like
Alice in Wonderland, who had eaten the little cake
with "Eat me" written on it in currants.

Now, she felt herself growing larger again. "I can't
run as fast as Jenny," Carey said. "Her legs are
longer. But I can run *pretty* fast."

"With a little coaching, you might run faster still,"

said Adam. "In any case, I'll call your parents, too, to see if they have any objections to your joining our junior track club."

"I don't have a mother," said Carey, still feeling a bit left out. "She's dead. She died when I was born. But you can call my father. His name is Thomas Cramer."

Adam did not say he was sorry to hear she had no mother. She rather wished he had. She did think, however, that he had a sad expression on his face as he wrote down her father's name in his little notebook.

After that, he walked with them out of the park and down to the street where his car was parked. It was a Volkswagen "bug" with a sunroof.

"I'm afraid I can't offer you girls a ride home. I have to pick up my wife at the doctor's office. She's having a checkup. We're having a baby, you know. But the walk will do you good. Best exercise in the world, walking. Strengthens the extensors and the triceps."

Folding himself up like a jack-in-the-box, Adam got in the VW. The top of his head, with its crop of curly, carrot-colored hair, stuck up through the sunroof.

Both girls looked after him as he beeped the VW's horn and drove off.

"He's so nice!" breathed Carey.

"And handsome, too," said Jenny. "I could tell from his voice. But you can tell me what he looks like if you want."

Carey described Adam as she and Jenny walked toward home. She also described some of the kids Adam was coaching. Booker was as brown as a polished buckeye. A girl, Maria, had coal-black hair and eyes shaped like triangular raviolis. The boy named

83

Walter had blue eyes and yellow hair. He had smiled at her.

All the rest of the kids, except for the girl with the tiny braids, she couldn't remember too much about.

After that, they discussed Adam's idea. They wondered what Jenny might wear on her head that would keep her in the right lane when she ran. Neither had any idea. But even guessing what it might be proved so interesting that they were more than halfway home before Carey remembered Aunt Richard's green pepper.

"I'll have to go back to Mr. Thrush's market and get it," said Carey with a worried air. "If I tell Aunt Richard I forgot, she'll think I'm not responsible. The market's just around the corner on the other side of the street." She was about to suggest that she would go faster if she went alone, when Jenny opened her watch and felt its face. "It's getting pretty late," she said. "Mama will worry if I'm not home on time. So I'll stay here while you hurry. My side hurts a little bit from all that running."

Carey had noticed that Jenny was flushed and a bit breathless. After all, she had run quite far in the park—and very fast. Since they had left the park, they had been walking and talking about a mile a minute.

"If you're sure you *want* to," said Carey. "There's a bench here to sit on. That's because a bus goes past here every morning to take people out to the university. It's got a sign on it that says 'Ferguson's Fine Furniture for Finicky Folks.' "

Jenny found the bench with her cane, but she did not sit down. "Maybe I'll go with you after all," she said. "My side doesn't hurt so much right now."

84

But Carey was already on her way. "Time me on your watch!" she called back. "See how long it takes me. Not more than five minutes, I should think!"

Before turning the corner, Carey looked back. Jenny was still standing, her cane held upright in her hand.

Carey was not back in five minutes. Nor in ten. It was more like fifteen minutes.

A fat woman with a pouch like a pelican under her chin was ahead of her at Mr. Thrush's fruit and vegetable market.

After pinching, sniffing, and handling practically every tomato, peach, melon, head of cauliflower or lettuce in the place, she finally completed her purchases and swept out of the store.

Although Aunt Richard had wanted Mr. Thrush himself to pick out "a nice green pepper" for her, Carey, to save time, had selected one. Plump and green and sweet smelling, it would do nicely. She handed it to Mr. Thrush. "My Aunt Richard says please to charge this pepper to her account. She will be in to settle her bill with you on Saturday."

"Not to worry!" said Mr. Thrush, popping the pepper into a small brown sack. "And here's a nice fresh bulb of garlic for her, with my compliments! If all of my customers were like Edna Richard, this would be a business to enjoy. But that one." He rolled his eyes in the direction of the departed customer. "Let me tell you . . ."

Carey knew that Mr. Thrush could, indeed, have told her more. He loved to talk. It would have been interesting, too. But with Jenny waiting for her she just said, "Thank you very much," and was out the door in a flash.

She ran very fast. She wished Adam could see her. He would want her on his team for sure.

She was sorry to have left Jenny alone for so long, though she knew Jenny wouldn't mind. Jenny would have things to tell her, because she always "saw" a lot with her ears and her nose. And, of course, she would have a lot to tell Jenny. She would tell her about the woman at Mr. Thrush's market who had a pouch like a pelican under her chin. She would mimic the way she had said, "Mr. Thrush, smell this cantaloup and tell me what you *think*."

Yoo-hooing, "Jenny, here I come!" Carey pounded around the corner on to Summer Street. She stopped suddenly. Jenny, who should have been sitting on the bench waiting for her, was not there!

Carey advanced slowly. Jenny might pop out any minute from behind a tree. But there were no trees. There was nothing to be seen but an empty bench with "Ferguson's Fine Furniture for Finicky Folks" painted on it.

Carey began to feel quite ill. Her heart fluttered as if a bird were caged in her chest. "Jenny!" she called in a quavery voice. "Oh, Jenny! Where are you?"

No one appeared but a paper boy, who was crossing a nearby lawn, folding papers as he came.

Carey ran to meet him. "Have you seen a blind girl about my age walking with a white cane anywhere around?"

"Naw," said the boy, "and I haven't seen any pink elephants walking around with a white cane, neither."

Carey squeezed her eyes shut to keep tears from

leaking out, but they came all the same. "Honest. I left her here right on that bench for just a minute. Well, maybe more than a minute, but not very long. When I came back, she wasn't there. I . . . I'm scared."

The boy spit out a blade of grass he had between his teeth. "You're not kidding, are you, sister?"

Carey began to blubber. "I, I wouldn't have left her. But we'd been to the park to play and she said she was tired."

"Well," said the boy. "I really didn't see her. But if she can play in the park and walk with a cane like you say, maybe she got tired of waiting for you and went on home."

"She *could,*" Carey sniffed, "though she's never been this way before."

"P'raps someone helped her," said the boy. "Blind people need a lot of help."

"Not Jenny," said Carey stoutly. "Jenny can do most anything."

"Then why worry," said the boy and went off, whistling.

Already Carey was beginning to feel more cheerful. The boy was right, of course. He had to be right. Jenny had just got tired of waiting and gone home by herself.

As Carey turned the corner onto Windermere Street, she saw Aunt Richard and Mrs. Lee standing in the side yard between the two houses. This was a little surprising. Aunt Richard always said she did not have time to "neighbor back and forth." "Neighboring back and forth" meant running into one another's houses drinking coffee. Though she graciously lent a cup of this or that to anyone who had "run out" of something, she would not borrow. Not even a green pepper. This did not mean she was not friendly with everyone. She even managed to get along with Pansy Prugh's mother, who, as far as Carey was concerned, was just a "grown-up" Pansy.

Something, however, had got Aunt Richard and Mrs. Lee together. And whatever it was, it had not made them happy. Aunt Richard looked stern, and Mrs. Lee's face was as white as if she'd dusted it with flour.

Once more Carey's heart began its birdlike flutter.

"Where is Jenny?" Aunt Richard and Mrs. Lee spoke in one voice.

"Isn't she here? I mean . . . I thought . . ." Looking at the two faces made Carey so frightened she could not go on.

Aunt Richard put a comforting arm around Carey's shoulders. "Try not to cry. Just tell us where you've been. Where did you leave Jenny? It's after five o'clock. For the last half hour Jenny's mother and I have been out of our minds with worry."

Sobbing, Carey told how they had gone to the park so Jenny could run free. There they had met Adam who was a track coach and he had said Jenny was a natural runner and he was going to figure out a way for her to stay in the right lane so she could run in track meets.

"Track meets!" exploded Aunt Richard. Though she was trying hard, between surprise, displeasure, and alarm she could not contain herself.

Mrs. Lee shook her head. "Let Carey go on," she said quietly. "I think she has more to tell. Go on, Carey. After you met this Adam person . . ."

"After that"—Carey licked at the salty tears that had run down into her mouth—"after that, we started home. We, we got a little way past Penwarden Road and I remembered your green pepper, Aunt Richard. I went back to get it . . ."

"Leaving Jenny alone?" prompted Aunt Richard.

"On a bench," whimpered Carey, as if this bit of information might make things a little better.

"You left Jenny on a bench to wait for you," said Mrs. Lee. Her voice was very calm. "Then when you came back from getting the green pepper, Jenny wasn't there. Is that right?"

"But she wanted me to leave her," said Carey, starting to cry again. "She didn't want to go because her side hurt from running so fast. And I wasn't gone very long . . ."

Mrs. Lee put her hand to her throat. "There could have been an accident. If Jenny were badly hurt, unconscious, she wouldn't be able to tell her name. I'd better call all the hospitals. The police—"

"I'll do that," said Aunt Richard, taking charge. In a crisis she turned from a worrywart into a commanding general. "You call Jenny's father."

To Carey she said, "Let's go home so you can get cleaned up a bit before your daddy gets home—and the police arrive."

8

"Not *Two* of Them!"

All the rest of that day and until far into the night when Carey finally fell asleep, cars passed in front of the Lees' house. Other cars circled the block. The people in the cars hoped to learn something more than the brief announcement heard on the six and ten o'clock news: A ten-year-old blind child, the daughter of Mr. and Mrs. John Lee of 6785 Windermere Street, was missing.

Jenny's mother and father had not left the house since Mr. Lee rushed home from the university. Carey's father, to whom the Lees had turned for advice, was working closely with the police. Aunt Richard, after having an attack of what she called "the vapors," had bounced back to complete efficiency. She had taken dinner over to the Lees' house, to "help out." She was in charge of everything.

No one mentioned the word *kidnapping*. Though no

ransom note had yet been received, it was on every-one's mind.

In a very special way, however, it was on the mind of Carey and that of Inspector Cosgrove, who was questioning her.

With Aunt Richard sitting on the sofa beside her, Carey didn't mind talking to Inspector Cosgrove. Even if Aunt Richard had not been sitting beside her, Carey would not have minded. Inspector Cosgrove was nice. He looked like a kindly old uncle. (Though Carey had no uncles of her own, she thought he looked like an uncle should.)

Shaped something like a teddy bear, he wore, de-spite the heat, a suit of teddy bear–colored tweed. His dark, deep-set button eyes were kindly as he said, "Now, dear. About this Adam you met in the park. Did he mention his last name?"

Carey shook her head. "He just said it was Adam."

"And he said he was a track coach? Did he say where?"

Carey tried to remember but all she could think of was "Adam."

"The other children who were with Adam in the park: do you recall any of their names?"

"Walter and Maria," said Carey, thinking hard. "And Booker and Carlos. There were some more I can't remember."

"Fair enough," said Inspector Cosgrove, making a little note on a pad of paper. "But now, let's get back to the time right after you left Mr. Thrush's market. You were hurrying, right? And you were a little wor-ried because you were later getting back than you thought you'd be."

91

Carey's chin quivered. "Y-yes."

"And as soon as you turned the corner you saw that Jenny wasn't on the bench or anywhere around?"

A lump came in Carey's throat she couldn't swallow up or down. It was all she could do to nod her head.

"Did you see anyone else? Talk to anyone?"

"J-just the paper boy. But he hadn't seen her, either." With these words Carey began to cry.

Aunt Richard, who had been sitting next to her, got to her feet. "Carey does not know the name of the paper boy. I have already asked her. She thinks he's a grade or two ahead of her at Clarkson School. In addition to that, Inspector Cosgrove, I think the child has answered questions enough for one day."

"I think you are absolutely right," said Inspector Cosgrove, and he came as near to making a bow as it was possible to make without making one. He put an arm around Carey's shoulder. "Don't worry, my dear," he said in his soft, furry voice. "We'll have your friend back safe and sound before you know it."

Neither Jenny's mother nor father felt Carey was at fault.

Sitting with them in their living room that night after the police had gone, Mrs. Lee said, "As soon as we accepted the fact that Jenny was blind, we determined she would be independent. That she would live the life of any normal, healthy child."

"That's why," added Mr. Lee, "we have always given Jenny all the freedom we thought she could handle. She began to learn to travel with a cane when she was only five. Everywhere we've lived, she's gone on errands in our neighborhood. We expected her to do the same here: go to school by herself, to the shopping center, and certain other places as soon as she knew the way."

Mr. Lee put an arm around Carey's shoulder and said, "The police will find her and bring her safely back. Wherever Jenny is, I know she's being brave. And we must be brave, too."

As Mrs. Lee gave Carey a hug and told her not to worry, she felt the wetness of Jenny's mother's cheek.

And that did not help at all.

Not being blamed, however, made Carey feel worse instead of better. Guilt lay like a big leaden ball in the pit of her stomach. She should not have left Jenny alone on that bench so far away from home. The only way to make up for it would be to get Jenny back.

But how? In the Linda Fairweather mystery stories, there were always clues. Linda, who spent her summers in interesting places like the Rocky Mountains, the seashore, or the north woods, always found them. To do so, she always went back to what she called "the scene."

The only scene Carey could think of was the bench on Summer Street where she'd left Jenny.

Her father had gone back to his office and Aunt Richard was napping when Carey left the house. No one saw her go.

And Carey saw no one as she turned on to Summer Street. The bench, with "Ferguson's Fine Furniture for Finicky Folks" painted on it, was just as empty as it had been the day before. Even so, she approached cautiously. That's what Linda Fairweather always did.

Linda Fairweather was always alert for any clues that might be destroyed or overlooked.

Carey sat down on the bench and looked around. The earth at her feet, bare of grass, was still a bit moist from rain that had fallen a few days before. It would have been a perfect place for Jenny to have printed a message in braille with the tip of her cane. But stare as she might, nothing was to be seen except the print of a very large shoe and an ant staggering under a load three times as large as itself. The shoeprint was pocked with small holes. She tried, but could not, make anything out of it in braille. Of more interest was the crumb. When the ant dropped it and continued on its way, she picked it up.

It proved to be actually larger than a crumb. It was a fragment of an ice cream cone—and a Bobbit's cone, at that! There was no mistaking one of Bobbit's cones. They were a dark, toasty brown and printed all over in a raised design of little squares.

Looking at the bit of cone made Carey think of Bobbit's fifty different varieties of ice cream. Thinking of ice cream made her think of the magazine with Mr. Lee's picture on the cover. She was still curious about that. There might even be a clue in it.

Carey thought a while before deciding that if there *was* a clue in the magazine, now would be a good time to find out.

When Carey got to Bobbit's, a young woman with a baby in a stroller and an elderly man were standing in front of the magazine rack, reading.

Carey had noticed this kind of thing before in other stores. People read magazines without paying for them and no one seemed to mind. Even the cashier herself was reading a new copy of *Ms* Magazine.

No one even looked in Carey's direction when she took a copy of *Newsmakers* magazine from the rack. On the cover, just as she remembered it, was the big picture of Jenny's father looking very dark and handsome. Beside his picture it said, "See Page 3."

Although the headline on page three was very large and black, the story was quite small. As there were no big words to slow her down, it took her no time at all to read:

John Talbert Lee III
Spurns Riches and Disappoints Father

John Talbert Lee II, one of the giants of the oil industry, is a disappointed man. His oldest son, John Talbert Lee III, has turned his back on the oil empire started by his grandfather. Instead, young Lee devotes himself to science. A modest man, he lives simply with his wife and two children in Riverville, Iowa, while doing research on DNA at Midwestern University.

Asked if he might disinherit his son, Lee Senior snapped, "No, of course not—though it wouldn't matter to him if I did. He's wealthy in his own right now."

The woman with the baby and the elderly man were still reading when Carey put the copy of *Newsmakers* magazine back on the rack. Although she carried enough money in her wrist purse to buy a cone, all taste for ice cream had vanished. In fact, she felt quite queer. A familiar figure was going through the door to the street. He was wearing a gray and white seersucker suit, shuffled as he walked, and was carrying a pink and white striped sack that quite obviously held a carton of ice cream.

Carey had never followed anyone before. She really didn't know why she was following the man in the seersucker suit, except it seemed the thing to do. He was the only clue she had to Jenny.

As Carey trotted along a dozen feet or so behind him, her mind replayed the conversation she'd had with him in Bobbit's less than a week before. "I could not help overhear part of your conversation. The gentleman whose picture is on the cover of the magazine is the father of this young lady?" To be polite, she had said yes. Then he had taken a good, long, hard look at Jenny and bought a copy of the magazine.

Not that he hadn't a perfect right to buy it. Or that he didn't have a right to stare at Jenny. People were always doing that. But still, there was something that made her keep following him.

Once, when the man in the seersucker suit had turned around to look behind him, Carey stooped and pretended to tie the lace in a shoe. If she caught up with him, she did not know what she would say.

With a little skip and a hop, she hurried on. The man, in spite of his shuffle, began to move faster. Then, just like that, he disappeared into an alley halfway up the block.

Carey ran.

At the entrance to the alley, she paused long enough

to see that the man was still in sight. He was running in a curious broken gait toward the dirty green van she had seen him in before.

As she turned into the alley, a warning voice in Carey's ear said, "Don't go down there!" but she did not heed it. "Wait!" she cried to the running man. "Wait!"

Reaching the van, the man paused with one hand on the door on the driver's side. "My dear," he said in the same soft voice Carey had heard before, "may I ask why you are following me? I find it most unseemly conduct in one so young."

"You stole Jenny," said Carey. It was not what she intended to say at all.

"I steal Jenny!" the man laughed, but there was no mirth in it. "Don't be ridiculous! Can't a man stop in an ice cream store and buy a quart of Karmel Krunch Pecan without being followed down the street by a child, a child with curly br—"

A sudden sound and he broke off his sentence. A policeman, smart in a new uniform, his club swinging at his side, went whistling past the entrance to the alley.

Though the policeman had not looked their way, the gray-faced man grew grayer still. "You're right, in a way," he said, in a voice that was almost a whisper. "The ice cream *is* for Jenny. Though I didn't steal her, I know where she is. I'll take you there. But you've got to keep your mouth shut on the way. Any hollering or bawling or yelling and the deal is off. Understand?"

"I guess," trembled Carey. Then, without knowing how it happened, she found herself being half-lifted, half-pushed into the high front seat of the van. A

97

second later, the gray man was in beside her at the wheel. "Head down and your mouth shut," he said, "or you won't see Jenny. Got it?"

The van throbbed into life. As it swung into reverse and scuttled down the exit to the alley, Carey raised her head a bit and said, "I'm going to yell, after all."

And she did. Although it was a good loud yell, from her huddled position it did not carry far. Even so, it was loud enough for a woman a quarter of a block away, walking with her husband, to stop and say, "I heard a child scream, Fred. I'm sure I did. It was a frightened scream."

"I didn't hear anything," said her husband. "And even if you did hear something, what could you do about it? You can't always go around poking your nose into other people's business."

"Any more yells like that out of you," said the gray man, "and you're going to be in serious trouble. Instead of helping Jenny, you're going to hurt her. I've already told you she's O.K. Right? And you're going to be O.K. Nobody's going to hurt you, either." His hands grasped the steering wheel so tightly, Carey noticed, that his knuckles looked quite blue. "All you're going to do is pay Jenny a little visit. Then the two of you will be going home. Right now, though, Jenny is waiting for her Karmel Krunch Pecan. If I don't hurry, I'll have soup on my hands."

Little by little Carey had inched herself up in her seat. By stretching her neck, she could see out the window. The shopping center and nice residential areas had been left behind. Downtown and the spa-

98

cious grounds of the university had given way to blank-faced buildings, derelict car lots, and junkyards.

Carey's heart began to pound as the van rattled across an old iron bridge and bumped its way across some railroad tracks. Empty freight cars, the legends on their side barely readable, stood about like over-sized children's toys. There were long, low, rambling buildings. There were tall, narrow ones. All were a dirty elephant gray and looked as deserted as the moon.

The gray man's attention was focused on the way that lay ahead. It could not be called a street or a road. It was simply a strip of dirty gravel, wide enough to allow the van to make its way between the ribbons of railway tracks and loading docks.

Once, when he peered into the rearview mirror, he passed one of his soft-looking white hands across his forehead. He was sweating heavily.

Carey inched up higher still. The gray man did not seem to notice until the truck passed over another series of railway tracks and came to a stop.

"Well, here we are," he said. A sigh burst from deep inside him. "No one's on our tail as far as I can see. And the ice cream, I trust, is not completely melted."

He gave two small toots on the van's horn, turned to Carey, and with a hint of a smile said, "Open, Sesame."

Then, with a great creaking and rumbling, one side of the big gray building opened before them. Carey sat up straight. Frightened as she was, she had to see what was going on.

The van bumped inside what looked like a great dark cave. The only light came from a flickering lantern.

The doors rumbled shut with even more noise than with which they had opened. From somewhere within a rasping male voice called out, "About time you were getting back. For the last half hour that young one has had me climbing up the wall. How her parents put up with a kid like that I don't know."

Carey slunk down in her seat as the gray man spoke. "I had a . . . I had a complication."

"What do you mean, 'complication'?" said the other suspiciously. "You've not gone and bloody well blown it, have you?" The beam of a flashlight coming out of the gloom played on the gray man's face.

"No, not that. Just a bit of a complication. It's just that . . . You see, I didn't have any choice. The kid was following me. There was a cop not more than a stone's throw away. I was afraid—"

"What are you trying to tell me, Deke?" The owner of the voice stepped near enough for Carey to get a glimpse of a thin, bearded face bordered on either side by shoulder-length dark hair.

Then the flashlight's beam dropped from Deke's white frightened face to Carey's.

"Oh, no!" said the Bearded One, stepping back in alarm. "Not another kid! Not *two* of them!"

9
In the Dark

"O.K., kiddo. In you go," said the Bearded One to Carey. "I'm afraid it's pretty dark in there. But you see, when we took over, er, rented this warehouse, we didn't think we'd be having *two* guests. With your little friend being blind and all, we figured it being dark in there didn't make any difference. But with you, kiddo, it's darker than the devil's pocket in that loft. You'd better take my hand."

Carey put her hand behind her, then, thinking better of it, let it fit into the man's dry and horny hand. After all, she had quit kicking and screaming so the Bearded One wouldn't carry her. Anything was better than that.

The dark that lay ahead was darker than any Carey had ever seen before. The flashlight the Bearded One carried cast a furtive light only a little way ahead. In its rays all she could see was the rough planks of the ramp they were walking on and the flooring that creaked beneath their feet when they'd reached the top. Motes of dust danced in its frail beams. Films of cobwebs brushed against her face.

Frightened, Carey peered ahead into the gloom. Curiously, at that moment, she felt she should be more frightened than she was. Jenny was there in the darkness. Somewhere. And she had come to rescue Jenny. Somehow. Then, wondering whether this was brave or foolish didn't matter anymore. For the flashlight had picked up a little nest of covers in one corner of the huge, dark loft. Sleeping in the middle of it was Jenny.

Carey knelt down. "Jenny," she whispered. "Wake up, Jenny. It's me. It's Carey."

Jenny sat up, rubbing her eyes. "Oh, Carey! Carey! I knew you'd come. I knew it! Did you bring Mom and Dad?"

The Bearded One noisily blew his nose. "I'll leave you two kids to it. I just don't want you to think for a minute this was *my* idea." Then he left, taking the flashlight with him.

Carey and Jenny, finished with hugging and crying, had not even started to talk before the beam of a flashlight again broke the darkness. " 'Most forgot your ice cream, my dear," said the voice of the Gray Man. "I'm afraid it's pretty badly melted. I'm also afraid we've only got one spoon."

"But is it Karmel Krunch Pecan?" asked Jenny.

"Of course, my dear. Exactly what you wanted."

"We can take turns with the spoon," said Jenny.

"I thought you'd work that out," said the Gray Man. "And I suggest after you've finished, you two little chickens go to roost." He started to leave, then came back, bringing the circle of light with him. "Don't think too badly of me, my dears. None of this was *my* idea."

There was so much to talk about they scarcely knew where to begin. But it seemed best to start with Jenny.

"You were gone a long time, you know. For a while, I didn't mind. It was kind of fun sitting there, listening to the world. There was a bird that kept saying 'Pee-a-wee' over and over, and there was a robin and a squirrel. Two buses went by, one each way. Then a nice lady stopped and wanted to know if I was all right, and I said I was. It wasn't until after she was gone that I started getting worried. I guess maybe it was the ambulance I heard. I walked up to the corner and listened to the traffic. When I came back, this man was there by the bench waiting for me."

"The one who shuffles?" asked Carey.

"Not him. The other one. He has a sad, whiny voice."

"He also has a beard," said Carey, for Jenny's information. "And quite long hair. But he does have a sad, whiny voice."

"Well, anyway," said Jenny, who was not too pleased to be interrupted. "He said he had bad news. He said, 'Your friend, Carey Cramer, has had an accident. She was hit by a car crossing the boulevard. It's pretty bad. She's in the hospital and asked for you.' "

"Oh, that was wicked of him!" cried Carey, "when I was perfectly all right!"

"I know," said Jenny. "But it was stupider of me to believe him."

"Well, anyway," said Carey. She did not want to think about how stupid *she* had been. She said, "Go on."

"We walked about a block, then he said, 'Here's my car. Get in. It's too far to walk to the hospital.' " Jenny's voice, which had been none too steady, quavered and broke. "And that was the dumbest thing of all. Mama and Daddy have told me about a million times not to get in a car with anyone whose voice I don't recognize. But I did, because I thought you were hurt."

"Did he say how bad?" said Carey. She was finding it very interesting to be talked about as if she were someone else.

"No. But I kept asking him. I asked him that, and I asked him if your father and Aunt Richard were there yet."

"Go on," breathed Carey.

"Mostly, when I asked him anything, he just grunted. He said Aunt Richard and your father were on their way, and that the doctors didn't know yet how badly you were hurt."

"But the Bearded One," said Carey, "who told *him* to come and get you?"

"He said he'd been visiting a friend in the hospital and was just leaving when a nurse grabbed him. She said it was an emergency and he was to go and get this blind child sitting on a bench and bring her to the hospital."

"I'd have known that was a lie," proclaimed Carey righteously. "Nurses don't do that."

104

"I know," said Jenny, beginning to cry. "But because you are my friend and I thought you were hurt, I believed him."

"Don't cry," said Carey comfortingly. "I did something just as dumb. I shouldn't have followed old Shufflefoot down that alley." With Jenny feeling so very bad, it only seemed right that she should confess.

And Jenny did, indeed, stop her crying. She listened carefully as she did when Carey read about Linda Fairweather, Girl Detective, in *The Mystery of the Secret Cove*. She did not say a word until Carey had finished telling about seeing Shuffle come out of Bobbit's carrying the pink and white sack, and all that happened after that.

"Mama and Daddy are going to be awfully worried if I don't come home soon. And awfully mad," said Jenny.

"My father and Aunt Richard are going to *kill* me," said Carey. Not until that moment did the awfulness of what she had done sink in. Instead of helping Jenny, she had made things worse. Very much worse, indeed.

There was plenty of room on the pile of old comforters for both of them. Worn out with crying, they fell asleep curled up side by side.

Carey, the first to waken, lay quietly. The silence was almost as frightening as the darkness. Earlier she had heard an airplane flying over. But now, except for her own and Jenny's breathing, there was no sound at all.

It was night. She knew that. When they had first put her in this place, there had been hairlines of light showing through from the outside. Now there was nothing except this total, stifling darkness. She put her thumb in her mouth for comfort, then as quickly took it out. Her thumb wasn't any good without her blanket. But even her blanket, with all its magic properties, could not get her and Jenny out of this predicament.

She got a terrible sick feeling in the pit of her stomach when she thought about what might still happen to them. Sometimes children disappeared and were never seen or heard from again.

She began to cry softly, not wanting Jenny to hear her. Jenny had been shut up lots longer than she had. She tried to figure back. From the time she left Jenny on the bench until she followed Shuffle from the ice cream store, a whole day had passed. That was easy. But how much time had elapsed since then, she had no way of knowing.

She thought about Aunt Richard waking up from her nap and calling, "Carey, love, where are you?"

And there would be no answer.

Aunt Richard's chin would quiver and her nose would turn pink as it did when she was worried or excited. She would take off her glasses, always shiny-clean, give them another polish, and say, "If anything has happened to that child while I was napping, I will never forgive myself." Her father would be sent for. He would come screeching into the driveway in his little white Fiat, slam on the brakes, and be out of the car in a minute. His face would be red and his eyes would flash. "My God!" he would say, "where is she? What have they done with her? If anyone has harmed

that child"—here he would swear most fearsomely—
"I swear, I'll kill him."

Carey thought about her mother, whom she hardly
ever thought about at all. Not because she didn't love
her, but because it was awfully hard to love a picture
in a frame. And she thought about God—whom she
hardly ever thought about, either—who was in a different kind of frame.

Her soft crying turned into a noisy sob.

Jenny sat up. "While you've been crying," she said
critically, "I've been thinking. I know something we
can do."

"What?" said Carey, sniffing.

"Explore."

"You can't explore in the dark," said Carey. Her
sobs were shocked into silence.

Jenny sighed. "I've told you about a million times
that dark doesn't make any difference."

"I know," said Carey lamely. Jenny had told her
that about a million times. But it was still hard to
understand. Just as it had been hard to understand
what Jenny meant when she had said, "Darkness isn't
like being blind. Closing your eyes isn't like being
blind, either. When *you* close *your* eyes, your eyes are
looking at the inside of your eyelids. And it's dark in
there. I don't see 'black' and I don't see 'darkness'
because I don't see anything at all except with my
mind."

With *her* mind going around like a top, Carey said
lamely, "I don't see how you can explore this place.
It's big. Bigger than fifty houses. Besides, you don't
know where anything is."

"Listen," said Jenny, sounding like a mother whose patience is strained to the breaking point, "if you know where things are, you're not exploring. Come on. I'll show you the listening spot. I've found that already."

The "listening spot" was a long way from the nest. How Jenny found it Carey did not know. Jenny said she had found it because she had nothing else to do, which sounded as good a reason as any.

It worked out very well. As Jenny pointed out, if you lay down on the floor and put your ear to this certain big crack, you could hear the men talking down below. "If they've got the radio on," added Jenny, "you can hear that, too. That's best of all, because if the news is on they'll talk about us."

The crack in the floor, however, through which both could hear, was also one through which Carey could see.

The two men sat close together on upended crates. Darkness was all around, except for a sputtering lamp placed on a third crate between them.

Shufflefoot was picking at the remains of a sandwich. "They should have the note by now. I hope to God they deliver the money right away so we can get those kids out of here."

"If they do pay the ransom right away," said the Bearded One, "who's going to collect it? I'll tell you one thing, it ain't going to be me. I did my part when I snatched the blind kid. From there on in, the whole thing's your idea. So I say, you pick up the money. If you hadn't spent all your time in prison in the library

108

reading all that fancy literchoor, we'd have hid out from the start—after all, we've got friends—and we would have stayed hid out. But, oh, no! You say we got to do it different. Like in that book you read, *The Purlined Something*. You say we got to get out every day and 'mingle.' And if we do that, you say, and act natural, the cops ain't going to suspicion us."

"Don't say 'not suspicion' us," said Shufflefoot in a cold voice. "Say the cops 'won't be suspicious.' And you'd be better off if you'd spent some time studying what you call 'literchoor' while you were in the pen."

"Aw, lay off it, will ya," whined the Bearded One. "I'm jittery, that's all. Nerves. We'll draw straws, just like we agreed we would. The short straw picks up the money just as soon as we get the word."

Other than to give each other a little pinch now and then, neither Jenny nor Carey had moved while the men were talking. But when Shufflefoot leaned over to turn on the radio that was on the floor between them, Carey could stand it no longer. As she hitched herself into a more comfortable position, one of the floorboards snapped like a firecracker going off.

Shufflefoot looked sharply around. "What was that? It couldn't be those kids, could it? Moving around, I mean? There are holes in that loft. If one of those young ones falls and breaks her neck, we'll be in real trouble."

"No bigger trouble than we're already in," said the Bearded One. "Kidnapping *two* kids instead of one. If they catch us we're apt to get the chair."

As he spoke, the radio announcer's excited voice burst through a crackle of static.

"This is a special announcement. Parents of ten-year-old blind Jenny Lee, kidnapped Thursday from a bench at Sixteenth and Summer streets, have received the ransom note for which they have been waiting. Details from Rick Rickover:

"Parents of Jenny Lee, missing since mid-afternoon Wednesday, have received a ransom note asking for $500,000 for the safe return of their blind child. Also missing since early afternoon today is ten-year-old Carey Cramer, friend and next-door neighbor of the kidnapped child." (Here, Jenny gave Carey quite a sharp pinch.)

"Although no ransom note has been received by the father of the Cramer girl, police have reason to believe the two kidnappings are connected. Fear is expressed for the safety of both children. Police say they are working on several strong leads—"

With an oath, the Bearded One reached down and snapped off the radio. "They tell us everything except what we want to know: how soon will they leave the money."

All that night Carey and Jenny took turns having bad dreams. When they awoke, both were cross and restless. Shufflefoot, usually so gallant, was not himself as he brought their breakfast. Doughnuts from the previous morning were dried out. The carton of milk was lukewarm.

After he went away, Carey and Jenny lay down on the pile of comforters side by side, bored with themselves and with each other. Carey remembered to ask Jenny how she knew her colors.

"Mom puts little bundles of stitches inside my

clothes where they don't show," said Jenny, yawning. "One little bundle for red, two for white, and three for blue. For green there aren't any bundles at all."

When Carey inquired about yellow, the answer was simple. Jenny said, "I hate yellow."

After that, time dragged by so slowly it was just as well that Jenny's watch had stopped for lack of winding.

There was no lunch.

They made an expedition to the listening spot when they thought it might be time for the six o'clock news. Carey could tell it was still daylight, because little rays of light filtered through the chinks in the ramshackle building. Peering through the crack in the floor, she could make out the shape of the van and of the two men huddled on their upturned crates. The radio was turned so low that Jenny and Carey, even with their sharp ears, could hear only a few words.

". . . ransom left in appointed spot in Green Meadows Park . . . remains unclaimed . . . police insist no traps have been set . . . urge kidnappers to take money and set blind child free . . . question remains, where is Carey Cramer. Still no ransom note . . ." The voice faded away in a crackle of static.

Carey and Jenny crept back to their nest.

When Carey awoke, she felt better. It was her first nap untroubled by bad dreams.

"Jenny?" she whispered. "Jenny, are you awake?" She reached out a hand and felt nothing. But she was not worried. Earlier, rain had pounded on the roof and cooled things off. But since then, hour by hour, it had grown hotter and more sticky. Instead of sleeping so close to Jenny that she could reach out and touch her, Carey had moved a few inches away. But now, wide awake and sitting up on the old quilt, she felt lonesome and frightened. She wanted Jenny close by. Crawling on her hands and knees, she didn't care who heard her call.

"Jenny! Jenny Anne!"

Not a sound was heard in the vast, silent warehouse. Carey could see nothing. Her mouth was so dry she could not swallow. It was a new kind of being afraid. Little grains of sand covered her tongue and lined her throat. She felt around in the darkness for the carton of milk. She hated warm milk, but even a swallow of anything wet would help.

Although she could not find the milk, the simple act of doing something helped her wits to return. Jenny must have gone to the listening spot by herself. There was nothing to do until Jenny came back. *She* had no cane. She could not walk alone in the dark.

When Jenny finally returned, Carey was too grateful to be cross. When she asked, half tearfully, "Where have you been?" Jenny pretended she didn't hear.

By nightfall, Carey's and Jenny's stomachs were growling hungrily. They had not seen either Shuffle-foot or the Bearded One since their breakfast of stale doughnuts and warm milk.

Even at the listening post there was a difference in the silence. Looking through the crack in the floor, Carey could see nothing.

No glimmer of light from anywhere. She sucked in her breath. It made a whistling, scary sound. "I don't think anyone's there, Jenny. They . . . they wouldn't

112

go off and leave us, would they, Jenny? They wouldn't go off and leave us here alone?"

Jenny's voice broke in a little sob. "I . . . I didn't want to tell you. I, I thought they might come back. But while you were sleeping, I found the way downstairs. The van was gone and the door . . . I couldn't open it."

Jenny was the practical one. Because Carey could not believe the Bearded One and Shufflefoot could be so wicked, Jenny led the way down the ramp into the dark cavern that was beneath them. There, Carey stood stock-still while Jenny stomped around with her cane and rattled the big warehouse doors in vain. There could be no doubt: the doors were locked and the men and van were gone.

"There's nothing here but three old crates," said Jenny, still stomping about. "And here's a sack with something yucky in it." An instant later, her cane struck a small, hard object in its path. There was a burst of static, and a newscaster's excited voice filled the air.

"With the ransom money still unclaimed, police late today found a green van believed to be the one used in the kidnapping of blind ten-year-old Jenny Lee, and possibly in the kidnapping of her friend, Carey Cramer. Road blocks have been set in all routes leading out of the county. Police in adjoining states have been alerted, as well as all citizens. The search now centers . . ."

The voice sputtered, faded, and then died.

"That's the trouble with batteries," said Jenny with disgust. "But at least we found out one thing. We

113

know that Shufflefoot and the Bearded One are gone for good."

"What are we going to do?" whimpered Carey, when they were back in the loft. "We can't stay here until we die."

"Explore some more," said Jenny, who was not afraid of the dark.

10
Good-bye, Bankie, and Other Matters

"You go this way," said Jenny, "and I'll go the other. That way we'll meet in the middle. But stay close to the wall. Keep touching it and you won't get lost. One of us may find something."

"What?" said Carey. She did not agree with the plan of separating at all.

"How do I know what we'll find until we find it," said Jenny crossly. "Let's start."

With her left hand touching the rough siding of the warehouse and her right arm outstretched like a shield, Carey shuffled along. She resented Jenny telling her what to do. Cross, hungry, and sleepy, she did not need light to tell her she was dirty. The smell of dust was heavy on her hands and clothing.

She thought about Linda Fairweather, Girl Detective. How would *she* like it, Carey wondered, if she had been locked up in a hot attic for goodness knows

how long? Just how would the great Linda Fairweather get out of a pickle like that? How would she
like it if she needed a bath, her teeth were fuzzy, and
her braids were flying apart? Linda Fairweather had
never in her life found a clue in the *dark*.

Just then, Carey's hand touched a round wooden
bar. Turning a bit, she faced the wall. Stretching
upward with both hands, she felt another bar just like
it! And like that, her resentment at Jenny vanished. At
last, all by herself, and in the dark, she had made a
discovery!

"Jenny! Come here. I need you!" she cried, not
realizing until later she had taken those words from the
mouth of Alexander Graham Bell.

But just as those words had brought Dr. Watson to
the side of Alexander Graham Bell, Jenny was at
Carey's side in no time at all. "What did you find?"
she demanded. "Tell me!"

"I don't know for sure," said Carey, "but I think it's
a ladder. Feel."

"It *is* a ladder!" cried Jenny. "And you found it!"

"But I don't know where it goes," said Carey,
beginning to feel some doubt.

"It goes up," said Jenny with confidence. "Hold my
cane."

You cannot say a person disappears in darkness,
thought Carey. A person can only disappear if you can
see him go.

Yet, Jenny disappeared in darkness. One minute she
had been standing by Carey's side, and the next minute she was gone. Then, from overhead, Jenny called
out.

"There's something up here at the top of the ladder. It's a kind of window, only there's no glass in it. If I can get it open . . ."

Then there was a pounding, which must have come from Jenny's fist, for a moment later she said, "Ouch!" More pounding followed, there was a loud, screeching sound of wood breaking, then a small swear word.

"It's open!" cried Jenny. "But before I go any farther, I'll have to have my cane."

"How am I going to give it to you?" Carey asked in a hollow voice. She already knew what Jenny's response would be.

"Climb up with it a little way," said Jenny. "You won't have to go very far. Then I'll reach down and get it."

"I need both hands to climb," said Carey, who had never liked ladders.

"You can climb a little way with one hand," said Jenny encouragingly. "Anybody can do that. After I have my cane, we can get out on the roof—I think. And after we're on the roof, someone is bound to see us. And as soon as someone sees us, we'll be rescued. We'll be on our way home. Come on up!"

With her left hand holding Jenny's cane and her right hand grasping a rung of the ladder directly above her, Carey groped first with one foot and then the other for a rung to stand on.

The ladder, however, turned out not to be like other ladders. It went straight up. Against the wall! After three rungs, Carey's heart was beating faster and her hand grasping the cane was so slippery she thought she would drop it.

"Here I am," said Jenny, right above her. "Hold it by the end and hand it up."

Leaning back to get in position, Carey thought she might fall. Then, as suddenly, she regained her balance.

Jenny said, "I've got it. Now you can come on up."

Carey climbed. It would have been worse to have stayed down below. She had not gone far before she had her first whiff of fresh night air. Then her head was through the opening Jenny had found, and she was breathing in great gulps of it.

"Don't be afraid," said Jenny, speaking like a mother to a child. "There's a little ledge out here to sit on."

There *was* a ledge. And it *was* little. Carey's legs dangled into space alongside Jenny's. But because there was nothing to see looking down, it was not as scary as it sounded.

Even so, it was better to look out across the night. On the other side of the river, the lights of the city were twinkling. Somewhere out there was her house. And Jenny's. Tears began to leak from Carey's eyes, and soon she would have drowned in pity if Jenny had not said, "We've sat here long enough. People will be able to see us better and we'll have a better place to sit if we're on the roof."

Roof! thought Carey. The perch on which they sat was narrow, but for her it was quite high enough. Jenny, however, was already moving away from her. In the faint shine from faraway stars, she could see Jenny was standing up. Carey followed. On her hands and knees.

*   *   *

119

"Do you think people can see us from here?" asked Jenny.

Carey was about to say, "When it gets daylight people can see us wherever we are," when a police siren wailed. The headlights of a car came bouncing over the railroad tracks. Farther away, another siren wailed. A parade of headlights was crossing the bridge.

"Are the sirens coming this way?" asked Jenny, who was now standing like the figurehead on a ship. "Are we rescued?"

"I *think*," said Carey. "Anyway, a lot of cars are coming. And a truck and a fire engine!"

The sound of the sirens drew closer. The first of the cars slammed to a stop. Others coming behind them did the same. The dark shapes of people poured out of them like figures in an animated cartoon. Headlights from the cars made the scene below almost as bright as day. And it was far noisier. Everyone seemed to be shouting and talking at once.

"How did all the cars and the fire engine know where to come?" shouted Jenny.

"Someone must have told them where to come," said Carey, her voice shaking with excitement. "The trouble is, they don't know where to *look*. The firemen are bringing axes. Some of them are carrying a log. It's big, bigger than a telephone pole. They're *running* with it. They're going to break down the door!"

"And when they do break it down," wailed Jenny, her voice almost drowned in the din from below, "and they do get inside, we won't be there!"

"I know," said Carey, "but maybe if we yell, maybe if we *scream*, they will hear us."

"You go first," said generous Jenny. "My voice is already tired from yelling."

Carey leaned out over the edge of the roof as far as she could safely go. "HELLLOOOOO!"

It was a good yell, as loud as she could make it. But amidst the crashing and banging of the firemen ramming the huge pole time after time against the warehouse door, no one looked up.

Jenny's "HALLLLOOOOO!" was a bit louder, but still no one heard.

"Maybe if we do it together," said Carey. "Ready, set, go!"

"HELLLOOOO!" and "HALLLOOOO!", one on top of the other, had scarcely died out when from down below came a delayed echo.

"What was that?" said Carey.

"I don't know," said Jenny, "but it sounded familiar."

As she spoke, the echo came again. This time, louder and shriller, it was followed by a penetrating cry. "Up there! Up there! Look! On the roof!"

Only one voice in all the world could sound like that, thought Carey. And she was right. Dancing around in the bold rays of the fire engine's headlights was Pansy Prugh. She was wearing her buttercup costume. With the yellow petals and green bodice.

Jenny was taken down the big fireman's ladder first.

Then it was Carey's turn. Slung over the back of a fireman like a bag of flour, and with one of his strong arms around her, she was not afraid.

On the ground there was such rejoicing! Jenny's parents were there, and Carey's father. And Pansy

Prugh and *her* father, who owned the newspaper and knew everything. There were also more firemen and policemen than Carey had ever seen in one place in her life, as well as newspaper reporters and photographers.

The only person missing was Aunt Richard, who had generously gone over to the Lees' house to stay with the baby.

Jenny had her picture taken alone over and over again. So did Carey. Then the two of them were photographed with Pansy Prugh. This was only right. Both knew that if it had not been for Pansy, they might have been on the warehouse roof for a very long time.

Inspector Cosgrove, warm and comforting, first questioned Jenny, then he questioned Carey. After that, he talked to them together.

They told him everything they could about Shufflefoot and the Bearded One. He said such descriptions made nice clues. He also said that one of the kidnappers—whether it was Shufflefoot or the Bearded One he did not know—had called police from a pay phone a short time before, telling them where the girls might be found.

Jenny and Carey felt better after hearing this. They couldn't believe that the kidnappers would have gone away and left them locked up in the warehouse to starve.

Inspector Cosgrove called every day to give a progress report. He said that the men, both of whom had gotten out of prison only a few months before, had gone "underground." This meant they were hiding out with friends. "But they won't get away with it forever," he added, "or my name is not Bartholomew P. Cosgrove."

Both Carey and Jenny hoped that Shuffle and the Bearded One *would* get away with it—though, of course, they dared not say this to Inspector Cosgrove. Between them, the girls agreed that the kidnappers, wicked as they were, had been very nice.

However, while the police continued their search, a good many other interesting things happened. For almost a week, pictures of Jenny and Carey (and Pansy Prugh) and stories about the kidnapping appeared in the *Riverville Daily Record*.

For the first time in her life, Carey looked for something in the newspaper beside the comic page. Everything she found of interest she read to Jenny.

A reporter and photographer for *Persons* magazine flew out from New York to take their pictures and interview them, but neither Carey's father nor Jenny's parents would allow it. They said enough was enough.

Jenny and Carey pretended to be disappointed, but they were not. They, too, had had enough.

It was also a lot more fun to go shopping for school clothes. Mrs. Lee and Aunt Richard took them to the big mall, where they found and bought identical jeans and shirts and Windbreakers. Carey watched with interest as Mrs. Lee made little bundles of stitches in hidden places so Jenny could tell what color her new shirts were.

Every day they practiced walking to school. Although Carey would usually walk to and from school with Jenny, Jenny wanted to do it perfectly by herself.

Then there was romance, romance far more exciting than the one between Miss Piggy and Paddington Bear.

Carey's father invited her and Jenny to dine with him and Sally Burns at a fancy restaurant. There, Carey and Jenny tried out all the different kinds of crackers that came in a gold basket and as a consequence were too full to eat their dinner. However, no one commented. Both girls liked being treated in this grown-up way. They both decided they liked Sally Burns and were pleased when she said, "Please call me Sally."

As if this were not enough, a few days later Carey's father gave Sally what he called a friendship ring, and Aunt Richard went out socially with Mr. Thrush.

Jenny came over to be present for the occasion.

Mr. Thrush, wearing a shiny blue suit, white shirt, and bow tie, did not look like himself at all. He came bearing a string bag of late summer vegetables: zucchini, squash, cucumbers, and Aunt Richard's favorite, green peppers.

Aunt Richard, her mustache newly removed, wore her Easter outfit, a dress of robin's-egg blue and a large flowered hat.

Before departing, Aunt Richard gave in and said Jenny could spend the night.

The next morning Carey and Jenny slept quite late. Twice Aunt Richard called them to say breakfast was ready, but they still lay in bed whispering and giggling.

After Aunt Richard called the third time, Jenny said, "In a little while when she comes upstairs to make us get up, let's pretend we're dead."

"Oh, let's!" said Carey.

Everything happened just as they planned. Presently, Aunt Richard did come upstairs to get them up.

When she tapped at the door and they did not answer, she came in the room. She stood for a moment looking at the two rigid but quivering bodies, then said, "The girls are dead. What a pity. That means they will not be wanting breakfast." Then, laughing softly, she tiptoed from the room, closing the door behind her.

"Aunt Richard," said Carey, "do you have a box?"

"What do you want it for?" asked Aunt Richard, who was in the kitchen snapping green beans, an early morning gift from Mr. Thrush.

"To put something in," said Carey.

"In that case," said Aunt Richard, who knew when not to push for information, "how big a box?"

"Like this," said Carey, holding her hands.

Aunt Richard went to a storage closet and came back with a box just about that size.

Upstairs, Carey got her bankie from under her pillow. She smoothed the bit of satin binding for one last time, then folded the remains as neatly as its unusual shape would allow.

Aunt Richard had finished with the beans and was in the garden snipping spent blooms from the marigolds when Carey took her box to the attic.

On the Saturday morning before school was to start, Jenny and Carey were weaving hot-pad holders on the Lees' porch when a red Volkswagen with a sunroof turned into the drive.

125

Carey jumped to her feet. "It's Adam! He's got that thing for you to run with. It looks like . . . I don't know what! It's weird!"

"Come, Mama, come!" cried Jenny. "It's Adam! He's got it!"

"We have a new baby at our house or I would have brought this sooner," Adam said to Mrs. Lee after greetings had been made all around. "But with all the commotion of the last few weeks, I thought I'd better wait until things settled down a bit. In fact, Inspector Cosgrove had some hard questions to ask of *me*." He grinned. "It seems he found one of my massive shoe-prints near the bench where Jenny was sitting when she was kidnapped. Lucky for me, one of the professors at the university was with me that morning while I waited for a bus. However, it didn't help that while I waited I was eating a Bobbit's cone."

"I saw your shoeprint, Adam!" said Carey. "But I knew it wasn't a clue."

"Good girl!" said Adam. "I'm glad someone was on my side from the start." He turned to Mrs. Lee. "I hope you and your husband are still of a mind to let Jenny go out for track."

"We're looking forward to it. As for Jenny, she's talked of little else."

"Well, this is the device," said Adam, showing Mrs. Lee the object in his hand. It consisted of a wide elastic band to which was attached a small box about the size of a package of cigarettes, an earphone, and a small antenna.

"Stand still, Jenny," said Adam. "Stop hopping around. I want to put this thing on your head."

Although Jenny did a poor job of standing still, Adam managed to fit the elastic band around her head. "We'll have something a lot better than this by spring; I've got this wizard friend I told you about working on it. But for now, this will do."

"Just what is it?" said Mrs. Lee. "How does it work?"

"It's the simplest kind of radio receiver," said Adam. "Someone, let's say Carey, stands at the finish line and with a sending unit broadcasts instructions, like 'move right' or 'move left' or 'carry on as you are,' and Jenny picks them up on her headset. Unfortunately, our little outfit has its problems. It's full of static, it may cut out entirely, or pick up other short-wave broadcasts. But with it, Jenny should be able to compete in all the school track meets next spring."

Carey's heart was beating fast as Adam turned from Mrs. Lee toward her. "I guess I don't have to tell you," he said, "that if you act as Jenny's eyes when she's running, you can't run yourself."

"I'd rather broadcast than run," said Carey.

"Good girl!" said Adam. "I've got your broadcasting equipment in the car. Now, if Jenny's mother approves, and your Aunt Richard says it's O.K., I'll take the two of you over to the park and try it out."

Mrs. Lee hesitated only for a fraction of a second before saying yes. It took Aunt Richard a bit longer.

That night, Carey went upstairs early to get ready for bed. She was tired from helping Adam. It had been a lot of work shouting "Right," or "Left, Jenny, left!"

or whatever, in order to keep Jenny on a straight course. And it was going to take a lot more work, according to Adam, as well as hours of Saturday practice, before Jenny could run without bumping into kids running on either side of her.

Fortunately, just as Jenny was beginning to get discouraged, on her headset she picked up a take-out order for sausage pizza with mushrooms. That cheered her up again.

Carey, teeth brushed and face washed, punched out "Good night" in braille and sent it across to Jenny on the hot line.

In a few minutes, Jenny's message, "See you tomorrow," came bobbling back in the coffee can.

After that, Carey got out the Bisness Book. She read through it, from the first entry to the one written just before Debra moved away. She remembered how sad she'd been when she had had to write "THE END."

Now, looking at the Bisness Book, she was not sad at all. It was hard to understand. Could it be, she wondered, because the entries were so silly they made her want to laugh? She thought not. For as she had read them, something other than their silliness was tapping at the door of her mind. Everything she and Debra had written had to do with seeing. Seeing Aunt Richard's mustache. Seeing Daryl Johnson go to the toilet behind the bush. Seeing Mrs. Purvis's lungs when she bent over. Seeing Chuck Smithers cheat on his math test.

Carey dug her fists into her eyes until the darkness was sprinkled with tiny rainbow-colored dots and streamers. Then she opened her eyes and looked around the room. With its white ruffled curtains, rose-sprigged wallpaper, her Bo-Peep lamp, her mother's picture, and all her books and other things, how pretty it was! She was glad she wasn't blind. Yet seeing with one's eyes wasn't the only way of seeing. Jenny had taught her that.

ABOUT THE AUTHOR

JEANNETTE EYERLY is widely known for her many novels about young people and their problems. Her books have been published in England, West Germany, Denmark and Finland. She has also contributed articles and fiction to major national magazines.

A graduate of the State University of Iowa with a Bachelor of Arts degree in English and Journalism, Mrs. Eyerly has lectured on art at the University and, with her husband, enjoys collecting art.

Mrs. Eyerly has long had a special interest in working with the blind and has served on the Iowa State Commission for the Blind. She does volunteer work taping books. She also has a strong personal interest in the fields of mental health, psychology and psychiatry.

Mrs. Eyerly and her husband live in Iowa and have two married daughters.